THE TYLER TWINS: SWAMP MONSTER

The Tyler Twins

SWAMP MONSTER

Hilda Stahl

WindRider BOOKS
Tyndale House Publishers, Inc., Wheaton, Illinois

First printing, June 1986
Library of Congress Catalog Card Number 85-52352
ISBN 0-8423-7626-7
Printed in the United States of America

CONTENTS

ONE
Horseback Ride

Terryl Tyler sat tall in the saddle and held the reins just as Gran had taught. What would her friends in Detroit think of her now, she wondered, if they saw her astride a spotted pony, following her new stepsister, Dani, along the riding trail through the woods? She hoped they wouldn't know that a tiny shiver of fear ran down her back as they rode deeper into the woods, or that sometimes she grabbed the saddle horn when the pony walked a little too fast.

She glanced over her shoulder at her sister, Pam, and it was like looking in a mirror. She and Pam were identical twins and in all their ten years no one had been able to tell them apart except Mom and Dad, and now Mom's new husband, David. Terryl frowned. David said he could tell the twins apart, but he wouldn't tell anyone how he did it. She wished she could figure his secret out.

Both girls had long honey-brown hair and dark eyes, and they were small for their age. Today they were dressed alike in Western hats, shirts, and jeans, with jackets that matched their jeans. Dani, David's daughter and their stepsister, was dressed almost the same way. Blonde curls peeked out from under her wide-brimmed hat and her eyes were as blue as the spring sky.

A twig snapped under Terryl's pony's hoof and she grabbed the saddle horn, looking around with wide brown eyes. "Dani, do you think we should turn back yet?"

Dani twisted around in her saddle. She had been riding horses all her life, so she wasn't afraid of falling off. "Are you girls tired already?" she asked, surprised.

"I'm not tired," said Terryl quickly. "I just don't want to run into those wild dogs your dad told us about." Mom's husband, David, was Dani's dad. Dani's mother had died when Dani was younger. Her dad had met the twins' mom when she moved into the area after the divorce. She and David fell in love, and were married now.

Terryl hadn't wanted that to happen; she had wanted Mom and Dad to call off their divorce and stay married. But they hadn't. So now, Dad lived in his plush apartment in Detroit and Mom lived with David, Dani, and David's parents on the Big Key Ranch near Thornapple, Michigan. The twins now lived nine months Mom and spent summers with Dad. Terryl was trying her best to adjust to it, but it was hard.

"I want to go back," said Pam, gripping the saddle horn with cold hands. "It's scary in these woods." She hadn't wanted to come on the ride, but Terryl and Dani had teased her until she finally had given in. Horses scared her, even the cute little pony she was riding.

"There is nothing to be afraid of," said Dani

patiently. "I've told you that over and over. I should know; I ride on this trail by myself all the time."

Pam looked deep into the woods and then up at the sky. She felt closed in and trapped. The fall leaves covering the trees blocked out the sun. "What about those dogs?" Her voice trembled and she flushed. She didn't want them to know just how frightened she was. Terryl hated it when she got scared, and Dani would probably think she was a big baby. Well, maybe she was. "I don't want those wild dogs chasing us." She lowered her voice to a mere whisper. "Or eating us."

Terryl agreed with her twin, but she wasn't about to let her know. "I sure don't hear any dogs." A twig snapped in the woods and she froze. She didn't dare look into the woods for fear of seeing green glassy eyes and wide snarling mouths with sharp teeth. Too bad Dani had made their dogs stay at the ranch.

Terryl relaxed slightly at the thought of the dogs at home. For their tenth birthday Mom had given her a big black and white Old English sheepdog named Malcom. He would've kept wild dogs away from her for sure.

Mom had given Pam a black cocker spaniel named Sugar, and Dani had a gold and white collie named Lassie. Terryl thought Malcom was the best dog, but she knew the other girls thought the same about theirs, too.

Dani stopped in a clearing and turned to wait for the twins. "We can rest here a while and play if we want to." She slipped easily off her pony. "Good girl, Lizzy," she said, reaching out to pat the pony's soft nose.

Terryl stopped her pony, then looked down at the ground. Could she get off without falling off? She gripped the saddle horn, swung her leg around and slipped to the ground without any problem. She stood up straight and tall and looked around to make sure Dani had seen her graceful dismount. But Dani was looking off into the woods with a worried expression on her face. Immediately Terryl forgot about showing off her dismount and peered through the woods with Dani. "What do you see?"

Pam jumped off her pony and almost fell under it, then scrambled over to the girls. "What do you see?"

"I don't know." Dani pulled off her hat and held it tightly in her hands. "I saw something, I think. Yes! Look!" She pointed at something bright among the dark tree trunks and the tangled bushes. "Do you see it?"

Pam moved closer to Terryl and held her breath.

"I see it," whispered Terryl, her mouth dry as cotton.

"Is it a dog?" asked Pam as she gripped her twin's arm.

"Dogs don't wear jackets," said Dani. She ran to the edge of the clearing and called out, "Who's there? Don't you know this is private property? Come here and talk to me right now!"

But no one came out and Terryl breathed a sigh of relief. She didn't want some strange person to confront them in the woods. "Let's go, Dani," she whispered, backing up with Pam holding tightly to her arm.

"I'm not leaving here until I find out who's watching us!" Dani ran into the woods and stopped near a giant oak tree that all three girls could've hid behind without being seen. "Answer me!" she called again. "Who are you?"

"Let's go with her, Terryl. We don't want her to leave us alone." Pam tugged on Terryl's arm and finally she nodded and they ran together after Dani.

"I see you!" shouted Dani, waving her arm. "I'm going to catch you!" She leaped around a bush and the twins followed. Deeper and deeper into the woods they ran until finally Dani stopped. The twins slid to a stop beside her and listened to the person running away, breaking twigs with loud snaps, like rifle shots. Dani turned to the twins. Her face was red and a twig had broken off in her curls. "Did you see who it was?"

"I didn't see anybody," said Pam.

"I saw a red jacket and that's all," said Terryl. "Besides, we wouldn't know anyone around here. We haven't been here long enough to know anyone but a few neighbor kids and some of the school kids."

Dani nodded. "That's right. I forgot. I wonder who it was. Why wouldn't he or she come talk to us?"

"Let's get out of here," said Pam, her face white and her dark eyes round and scared.

"I think Mom would want us to get right back," said Terryl. She knew Mom and David had gone to Grand Rapids shopping, but she didn't want Dani to think she was afraid. After all, Pam was the scaredy-cat of the family; everybody knew that.

Just then a loud shout came from the clearing, then the sound of pounding hooves. Someone was chasing the ponies away!

The girls stared at each other for one wild minute, then dashed for the clearing. The ponies were gone and no one was there. A ground squirrel zipped under a pile of dead leaves and a bird called high in a tree.

"This is not funny!" shouted Dani with her hands cupped around her mouth. "Whoever you are, you come here right now! I mean it! You're not scaring us."

Terryl and Pam disagreed; they were more frightened than they'd ever been before. If they could move, they'd run down the trail to the ranch and never step a foot out of the Big Key's yard again!

Suddenly Dani darted forward. "I've got you now!" she cried, as she dashed into the woods.

Terryl pulled off her hat and stood with trembling legs, twisting the wide brim up against the crown. *How can Dani be so brave?* she thought, then frowned. Usually *she* was the bravest person around and did all the things that other kids were afraid to do. But here in the country she felt like a girl from outer space or something.

"Look who I found!" shouted Dani. She yanked and pulled out from behind a clump of bushes a short, plump girl with a black cap of hair, angry blue eyes, and a nose too big for her small face who was dressed in too-tight a sweater and jeans.

"Sarah James!" cried the twins together. Sarah lived across the road from the Big Key Ranch and she loved to make trouble for the girls.

"What are you doing here?" asked Dani, standing with her hands on her hips and her chin thrust forward.

Sarah tugged her sweater down, but it popped right back up, showing a line of pink skin. "I told you I wanted to come with you."

"We said you couldn't," said Terryl. "You can't play with us and you know why."

Sarah crossed her plump arms over her chest. "You can't stay mad at me, you know. I said I was sorry for wrecking your mom's plants in her greenhouse. I said I was sorry and that means you have to forgive me and stop being mad. You have to because you're Christians. So there!" She bobbed her head and her cap of black hair bounced.

Terryl peeked at Dani and Pam. Both of them had accepted Jesus as their Savior, but she hadn't. Right now she didn't want to talk about it or think about it. She'd rather think up a great plan for getting even with Sarah James for destroying Mom's little baby plants. Mom had worked so hard to keep the plants alive. She had always wanted a greenhouse and a garden, and now that she was married to David she could have all of them that she wanted. But Sarah had broken into Mom's greenhouse and destroyed her plants in anger. Terryl narrowed her eyes and studied Sarah. Somehow she'd make Sarah sorry for what she'd done.

TWO
Sarah's Mean Trick

Sarah stood before the twins and Dani with her eyes narrowed, her round cheeks burning. "I told all three of you that I wanted to come with you. I told you I wanted to play, didn't I? I told you as soon as Saturday morning cartoons were over that I'd come to your house. I told you! Didn't I?"

Terryl stepped forward with her fists doubled at her sides. "And we told you that you couldn't come over. We didn't want to play with you today. We didn't want you hanging around us."

Sarah shook a stubby finger at Terryl. "Don't you dare talk to me like that, whichever twin you are! I'll tell your mom on you. I'll tell everyone that lives in your house on you!"

Gran and Grandad, Mom and David, Diane the housekeeper, the twins, and Dani all lived in the gigantic ranch house and Terryl knew Sarah had a big enough mouth to tell everyone every detail of what bothered her.

"Go right ahead and tell," said Pam with a toss of her long hair. "They are all mad at you for what you did to the greenhouse."

Sarah sagged in defeat and she stepped back a step. "That sure doesn't seem right to me. I'm just a poor little girl without any brothers and sisters and all I want is to play with you girls. I can't believe you'd treat me this way." She squeezed out one lone tear, watching each girl for any sign of guilt.

"Cut it out, Sarah," said Dani with a frown. "That little act won't work with us."

"What act?" she asked, her eyes wide in pretended innocence.

Dani turned to the twins with an exasperated sigh. "We'd better get the ponies and get home."

Pam looked all around. "Where are they?"

"I chased them away!" Sarah folded her arms and looked very smug.

"And you ran into the woods and made us follow you, didn't you?" Terryl stepped right up to Sarah. "You think you're so big! You think you can make us play with you! Well, you can't! I just wish we'd let you run through the woods and get lost." Just then Terryl noticed Sarah's blue sweater and further words died in her throat. She tugged at the blue sleeve. "Where is your red jacket?"

"What red jacket?" Sarah snapped, pulling away. "I wore this sweater."

Pam gasped. She and Dani looked at each other, then they both looked at Terryl. "There must be someone else hiding from us in the woods," whispered Pam. Shivers ran up and down her spine. "Sarah, who came to the woods with you?"

Sarah smoothed down her sweater sleeve. "Nobody came with me. I told you, I don't have anybody to play with today except you girls."

Terryl looked off into the woods. "I bet there's an escaped convict out there." She'd seen something like that on TV. "I bet there is!"

"What?" cried Sarah.

"What?" cried Dani and Pam together.

They all looked at Terryl and she flung her arms wide. "He probably saw us coming and he wanted our ponies to get away on. He might come back and slit our throats and bury us right here where no one will ever find us!"

Pam shivered, then flushed with embarrassment. Terryl was only making up a story to scare them. Terryl loved to be dramatic about everything. "It was probably only someone out for a walk, Terryl."

Terryl shrugged. "Maybe so. But I could be right, you know."

"We have to find the ponies," said Dani. She walked into the woods. "Lizzy! Where are you, Lizzy?" she called. "Come here! Come on, Lizzy!"

Deeper in the woods they heard Lizzy neigh and a minute later she ran around the trees toward Dani. The other ponies followed, their reins swaying.

"Good girl, Lizzy." Dani rubbed Lizzy's spotted neck. "You're a good girl."

Terryl and Pam stood back and waited for Dani to lead their ponies to them. Pam wanted to walk home, but she didn't say anything. Slowly, awkwardly she stuck her foot into the stirrup and swung her leg up and over the saddle. She clung to the saddle horn and the reins, watching Terryl rub her pony's neck and talk to it.

"Who do I ride with?" Sarah stood with her fists on her hips.

"You walked here, you can walk back," snapped Terryl.

"You can't ride with me," said Dani.

Pam wanted to let Sarah ride with her, but she knew Terryl and Dani would get mad. "I'm riding alone," she said quietly.

Sarah suddenly reached up and broke off a switch from a young maple, then ran at the ponies. She yelled at the top of her lungs, swinging the switch and slapping it at the ponies. They leaped away in fright, dumping Dani and Terryl on the ground. Pam screamed as her pony bolted, and she held on to the saddle horn in terror. Her pony dodged around a bush, unseating Pam who flew over the saddle and landed with a loud thud.

"Pam!" Terryl ran toward her twin, feeling the pain of the fall just as if she'd fallen herself. Fear pricked her skin and she dropped down beside Pam and lifted her head. "Pammie! Are you hurt?"

Pam groaned, but managed to sit up. She rubbed her shoulder while Terryl brushed dirt and leaves off her. "I think I'm all right," she said weakly, but she knew she'd never in all of her life get on another pony. Let Terryl and Dani ride all they wanted, but she was not going to.

"Can you stand, Pam?" Dani carefully helped Pam up, then all three of them turned to face Sarah James.

Sarah lifted her round chin and stared back at them. The switch fell from her hand and landed near her feet. "Well, why are you staring at me? You asked for what you got!"

Terryl walked toward Sarah and all the color

drained from Sarah's face. "You hurt my sister!" Terryl said in a cold, angry voice. "My twin sister! My identical twin sister!"

Sarah stepped back, stumbled over a tree root, and plopped to the ground. She stared up at Terryl with fear in her eyes.

"Leave her here and let's go find the ponies," said Dani.

Pam nodded, and spoke to Terryl. "We don't want to do anything to Sarah that we'll be sorry for later." What she really wanted was to pick up the switch and use it on Sarah, but Pam knew Jesus didn't want her to do that. Jesus wanted her to love Sarah, even if it was hard to do so.

Terryl narrowed her dark eyes thoughtfully and then she grinned. "Yes. We'll leave her here for the wild dogs."

Sarah gasped and perspiration popped out on her face. "Wild dogs?"

Terryl nodded. She knew Sarah was terrified of dogs. "David told us to stay on the trail so we wouldn't get attacked by the wild dogs that he saw out here." Really the wild dogs were in the state property that bordered the Big Key, but Sarah didn't need to know that. "We are going to leave you here all alone, Sarah James, and someday we'll come back for your bones."

Sarah sprang to her feet. "Don't leave me here! Please! I'm sorry about hitting the ponies. Let me stay with you. Please, please, please!"

Terryl continued smugly. "We might not even find your bones. Dogs eat bones, you know."

Sarah slapped her hands over her face and groaned.

"Don't, Terryl," said Pam.

Terryl stared at Pam with her mouth open. Pam had never tried to stop her before. But somehow Pam was different here at the Big Key; she even liked having a room of her own, instead of sharing one with Terryl. They'd *always* shared a room. Terryl frowned at Pam, wondering if one of these days Pam might even try to boss her around. "I'm not doing anything to her," snapped Terryl.

Pam's face turned brick red and she lowered her eyes.

"You are teasing her," said Dani. "And Dad says teasing can hurt as much as punching her in the nose."

Terryl flipped back her honey-brown hair. "What does your dad know? Besides, he's not my dad and I don't have to listen to him."

"Oh, yes, you do!" Pam looked Terryl right in the eye. "And you know you do! He's our dad, too, now."

"Terryl needs two dads to make her mind," muttered Sarah.

"Did you say something?" Terryl glared at Sarah, who cringed and shook her head.

Dani tugged on Terryl's arm. "Come on. We have to find the ponies and get home before our parents start worrying about us."

Terryl sighed and watched a robin fly from one tree branch to another. "All right, let's go. But I don't want Sarah to go with us."

Dani glanced at Sarah. "She'll have to stay with us or she might get lost."

That gave Terryl a brilliant idea. They would lose Sarah in the woods. She deserved it after what she'd done. Terryl caught Sarah's plump arm and tugged. "Well, come on, Sarah. If you're coming with us, let's get going! We don't want to be here after dark, you know!"

Sarah tugged free and rubbed her arm, then finally fell into line with the girls.

In the distance a dog barked and Terryl's stomach tightened in fear. What if the wild dogs were out there? She wanted to tell Dani to turn back, but she pressed her lips together and didn't say a word.

A pony whinnied and Dani ran toward the sound with the other girls close behind her.

Terryl stumbled over a vine and almost fell, but caught herself against the rough bark of a tree. Her chest rose and fell as she fought to catch her breath. Up ahead she saw Dani and Pam disappear behind a clump of trees. Behind her, Sarah stumbled over a root and sprawled to the ground. Quick as a flash Terryl dodged behind a tree and peeked out at Sarah as she slowly stood, then looked around.

"Where are you, girls?" she called nervously.

Terryl bit back a giggle. Pam and Dani would think that she was taking care of Sarah. Well, that's just what she was going to do. She shrank back against the tree and stood very still. Finally Sarah started running, but in the opposite direction of where Dani and Pam were. Sarah was going to get lost, and it served her right!

Terryl swallowed hard and pushed back the twinge of guilt that suddenly hit her, then ran after Dani and Pam.

tHREE
Lost in the Woods

Terryl saw Pam's blue denim jacket through the trees and ran to catch up to her. Sarah's loud cries followed her for a few moments, but Sarah suddenly quit shouting. Abruptly Terryl stopped and looked in the direction that Sarah had gone. There was no sight or sound of the big sassy girl. Fear and concern momentarily touched Terryl's heart, then she shook her head and ran to catch up with Pam and Dani.

Pam looked over her shoulder as Terryl approached. "Terryl, where's Sarah?"

Terryl shrugged. "I thought she was with you." The lie burned her tongue, but she wouldn't make it right.

Then Dani spotted the ponies and ran faster toward them. They spooked, kicked up their heels, and galloped away until they were out of sight once again. With a tired sigh Dani stopped and sank against a tree.

The twins ran to her and dropped to the ground to rest as a squirrel scolded them from a nearby treetop.

"Let's go home," said Pam, gasping for breath. She pulled off her jacket and tied the sleeves around her waist. Her hat settled down between her shoulder blades and the string pressed against her throat. "I want to go home, Dani. Gran will come find the ponies." Gran trained all the horses on the ranch, and took care of them.

Dani pushed her hat to the back of her head. *"I'm responsible for the ponies. I have to find them and take them back on my own."* She shot a look around. "Where's Sarah?"

"Isn't she with you?" asked Terryl as innocently as she could.

"Where is she?" Pam's voice rose in concern. "We can't let her get lost."

Dani cupped her hands around her mouth and lifted her chin high. "Sarah! Sarah, where are you?" She listened, but heard nothing. "This is really terrible. What could've happened to her?"

Pam rubbed her damp palms down her jeans. She glanced at Terryl, and she knew. She and Terryl could often tell what the other was thinking or feeling; Mom said it was because they were identical twins. "What did you do to Sarah, Terryl?"

Terryl forced back a guilty flush. "What do you mean, Pam?"

"Don't try to sound innocent! It won't work with me and you know it."

"If you know so much then figure out for yourself where Sarah is," Terryl said angrily, and jammed her hands into her jacket pockets. She lowered her eyes so Pam couldn't read her thoughts.

"Don't do this, Terryl," said Dani softly as she touched Terryl's arm. "Something terrible could happen to Sarah. She might run into the swamp.

Grandad said that once a team of horses pulling a wagon drove into the swamp and just disappeared."

Pam gasped and the color drained from Terryl's cheeks.

Dani swallowed hard. "And we did see a trespasser. It could be someone dangerous and he might have Sarah right now. If you know where she went, we have to follow her and find her."

"Terryl?" whispered Pam.

"Oh, all right! She ran off that way," Terryl pointed in the direction she'd seen Sarah run. "But I don't think she'll go far without us."

"Let's go!" Dani sped through the trees, dodging in and out and around the bushes and undergrowth, yelling. "Sarah! Sarah, where are you?"

"Sarah?" Terryl called.

"Sarah!"

Suddenly Dani stopped and the twins almost collided into her. "This is the end of Big Key property. Over that creek is State land. It's too dangerous to go there by ourselves. There are all kinds of swamps, and those wild dogs, too."

"Then we'll have to go home," whispered Pam. Suddenly she wanted to be out of the woods and in the open field near the ranch house. She wanted Mom and her dog, Sugar. She hated the rustling noises in the woods and the thought of the wild dogs and the swamp that ate horses and wagons.

"We can't leave Sarah," said Terryl in a low, tense voice. She hadn't wanted to hurt Sarah, only scare her a little.

"No, we can't." Dani rubbed perspiration off her

forehead. "We'll have to go on State property. But we'll have to be very, very careful." She shivered. "Terryl, Pam, stay right behind me no matter what happens."

"I don't want to go," whispered Pam.

"It's too dangerous to stay here alone," said Dani.

"Let's just hurry up and find her so we can go home," said Terryl. She hoped the girls weren't blaming her for their trouble. It would hurt too much to have them mad at her.

Carefully Dani jumped over the creek, barely making it to the other side without getting her boots wet. She turned and waited for the twins. "Make a running jump, girls."

Pam took a deep breath, then ran toward the creek. She jumped and landed on the other side, lost her balance and fell to the ground, her hands sliding through the sodden leaves. She pushed herself up, her face red, and wiped off her hands and knees. "I made it," she said with a sheepish grin.

Terryl hiked up her jeans and ran for the creek. She leaped up and sailed through the air. When she landed her foot slipped and her boot slid down into the muddy, cold creek. She jerked up her leg to find her boot covered with mud and slime. She wrinkled her nose and shook her foot. Mud flew around and Dani and Pam jumped back before it hit them. Terryl picked up a handful of old leaves and rubbed off her boot. *Pam and Dani must think I'm really dumb to miss such an easy jump*, she thought in disgust. She peeked through her thick lashes at them but they were both looking further into the woods. With a tiny sigh she dropped the leaves, squared her thin shoulders, and lifted her chin. "Let's find Sarah."

"I thought I saw something move over there," whispered Dani, pointing.

Terryl squinted and tried to see more than tree trunks and bushes and birds. "Was it Sarah?" Terryl kept her voice low just in case it wasn't Sarah.

Pam locked her icy hands together and strained her eyes to see whatever Dani had seen.

"I guess it's nothing," Dani said and strode forward, watching around her and where she stepped.

They walked a few steps, then stopped and called to Sarah. They walked further and called again, always listening for an answer.

"We've come a long way," said Terryl after a while, looking around. All the trees looked alike to her and there was no path to follow.

"Sarah!" Dani shouted. She sounded desperate and frightened. "Sarah, answer me if you can hear me!"

No sound came back other than the usual noises of the forest. Where could Sarah be, and why couldn't she answer them?

"What if she went back home?" said Pam. "She could've, you know, and she wouldn't tell us. She's probably waiting right now for us to walk into the yard so she can laugh at us."

Anger shot through Terryl. "I bet she did go home."

Dani nodded. "You could be right. Maybe we should turn around and go back."

Just then, a cry like nothing they'd ever heard before rent the air. The girls screamed and grabbed for each other and stood huddled together, trembling with fear.

"What was that?" whispered Terryl and Pam together.

"I don't know," answered Dani. "But I'm getting out of here now!" She pulled free from the twins and spun around, then stopped and stared. Sarah James stood just inches away, her face white and her eyes round with fear. "Sarah!" Dani exclaimed.

"Sarah!" echoed the twins.

"What . . . what was that?" Sarah's voice shook and she looked ready to faint.

"Where were you?" asked Terryl, suddenly suspicious.

"What was that noise?" Sarah repeated, tugging on her sweater with trembling hands.

Terryl grabbed Sarah's arm. "Where have you been?"

"Yes, where?" asked Pam.

"Answer us!" cried Dani, her face red and her fists doubled at her sides.

Sarah looked at Dani, then Pam, and finally Terryl. "I . . . I followed you." The last word was barely a whisper.

"Followed us!" the girls cried in unison.

Sarah stumbled back from them, her hands out protectively. "Don't be mad. I was only getting even with you."

Dani threw up her arms and turned away in anger. Pam stared at Sarah and shook her head in disbelief. Terryl leaped on Sarah and sent her flying to the ground. She pinned her shoulders to the ground and straddled her.

"You made us come on State property where there are wild dogs and awful swamps! How could you do that?"

Tears filled Sarah's eyes and ran down the sides of her round face. Terryl groaned and jumped up.

"You're a big baby, Sarah!" Terryl said angrily. She rammed her hands in her jacket pockets and hunched her shoulders.

Dani shook her head in disgust. "Let's go home," she said.

"What about the ponies?" Pam hoped Dani would go home without them.

"We'll look for them on the way home," answered Dani, pulling a twig from her blonde curls.

Sarah got up and walked close to the girls. "What was that terrible noise?" she asked again, just above a whisper.

The twins looked at Dani, expecting an answer; she seemed to know everything about living in the country.

Dani wet her dry lips with the tip of her tongue. "I don't know what it was, but I don't think we should wait to find out."

Terryl turned slowly, looking all around them. Finally she turned back to Dani, who hadn't moved. "What are we waiting for? Let's go home."

Tears filled Dani's wide blue eyes and she looked helplessly at the girls. "I don't know which way to go," she whispered.

Terryl's heart sank and she stared at Dani in horror.

four
The Swamp Monster

Suddenly Pam grabbed Sarah by the shoulders and
shook her until her head bobbed back and forth.
"How could you do that to us? Now, we're lost and
we might never find our way home!"

"You're hurting me! Twin! You're hurting me!"
shouted Sarah.

Terryl stared at her twin with her mouth hanging
open. Pam had *never* attacked another person in
her life! A strange feeling ran over Terryl and she
gulped. Everything was getting so confused. Pam
was acting like a totally different person . . . and
that frightened Terryl. She reached out and grabbed
Pam's arm, then roughly pulled her away from
Sarah.

"Stop it, Pam!" she shouted in anger and fear.
"Just stop it right now!" Pam turned heatedly and
for a moment Terryl thought her sister was going to
hit her. But then she stopped, letting her hands fall
to her sides.

"I'm sorry, Pam," Terryl explained shakily. "I had
to grab you so hard because I thought you were
going to beat up Sarah, or hurt her."

Pam grinned sheepishly. "I thought I was going to,

29

too. I guess we do act alike sometimes, don't we?"

Terryl rolled her eyes. "I guess we do!"

"Are you girls ready to go?" asked Dani dryly.

"I am," Terryl said.

"Me, too," said Pam.

"You're both mean and crazy," said Sarah, rubbing her arms. "I'm glad I'm not twins."

"So are we!" Terryl, Pam, and Dani all said at once in the same relieved way. Then they looked at each other and laughed.

"Well, I don't see what's so funny," said Sarah.

They laughed harder, then suddenly another terrible cry like the one they'd heard earlier split the air. The girls screamed and clung together, and Pam and Sarah burst into tears. Dani and Terryl pulled away and looked all around.

"It's a swamp monster," whispered Terryl. "I saw a story on TV about a swamp monster."

"Did it look like a giant lizard?" asked Dani with a shudder.

"Yes. A giant lizard that ate people."

"I want to go home!" cried Sarah. "I don't want no swamp monster to eat me!"

Pam knuckled away her tears and took a deep breath. "There is no such thing as a swamp monster. That TV show was all make-believe and you know it, Terryl!" Pam didn't want to admit it, but a part of her believed that the cry had come from a swamp monster. But the logical part of her knew it wasn't true. Pam was a lot like Mom—logical and down-to-earth—not dramatic and creative like Dad and Terryl. "Now, stop trying to frighten us with swamp monster talk!"

Terryl snapped her mouth closed and didn't say another word. Pam really was different than she had been before they came to the Big Key in September. Terryl wondered how long it would take her to get used to this new side of her sister.

Pam narrowed her eyes thoughtfully as she looked around. "We have to start walking, girls. Dani, what would be the best way to go?"

Dani looked around, then up at the sun, which was behind a thin layer of clouds. "We know we have to jump back across the creek. But where is it?"

"Over there!" cried Sarah, pointing. She ran toward it and the others followed.

"I don't see our footprints from before," said Dani with a frown.

"Who cares!" cried Terryl. "Let's jump across and get out of here." She jumped and easily made it across. This spot was narrower than the other place they'd crossed.

Pam jumped across and walked toward a clump of bushes that she was sure she'd seen before. As she walked the ground became spongy. She glanced down to find water oozing up around the soles of her boots. No one else seemed to notice, so she shrugged it off and kept walking with the girls.

Suddenly Dani stopped. "Don't take another step, girls!" She looked down at her feet and as she watched one boot sank down until the toe was covered with mud.

"What's wrong?" asked Terryl.

"I'm not standing around waiting for the swamp monster," said Sarah as she walked away from the girls. "Coming? Or do I have to lead the way? I might be able to get us out of here. I'm just as smart as you, Dani!"

"Sarah, stop!" screamed Dani.

Sarah stopped dead at the tone of Dani's voice, and the color drained from her face. "What's the matter?" she asked.

"We're in the swamp," whispered Dani hoarsely.

Pam gasped and the world seemed to spin around. She blinked and then opened her eyes wide to force back the dizziness. "What are we going to do now?"

"Turn carefully and walk back the way we came," said Dani. She picked up her foot and her boot popped out of the muck with a loud smack.

"I'm scared!" Sarah stood rooted to the spot, her arms out and her tennis shoes slowly sinking.

"You come here right now!" cried Pam, shaking her finger at Sarah. "We will not walk over there and pull you out when you sink in up to your eyes!"

Terryl looked at Pam with new respect, then slowly followed her footprints back to solid ground. She wiped the sweat off her face and waited for the others. She watched as they picked their way carefully over the ground, then breathed easier when everyone was safe beside her.

"That was close," said Dani, wiping her arm across her face. "Each of us must find a stick and use it to feel our way. Somehow we have to get out of here."

"I'm glad we have angels watching over us," said Pam. Mom had just read the Scripture that morning that said God sent angels to watch over his little ones.

"I wish my angel would pick me up and carry me out of here," said Sarah. She glanced around as if she was looking for her angel, then found a heavy stick and picked it up and held on tight.

Terryl felt funny thinking about angels watching over her, but she was glad they did. She found a heavy stick, too, and picked it up and poked it into the ground ahead of her. If the stick sank in mud, she knew not to walk there. If the stick wouldn't go into the ground, she knew it was safe.

The girls walked along in silence, feeling their way. Birds sang overhead and squirrels chattered. Small animals ran through the underbrush, scurrying to get out of the way. Pam wondered if the others were thinking about the swamp monster and listening for the terrible cry. She hoped she never heard such a cry again.

"Stop!" Dani stood with her stick held in her hand like a staff. She waited until the others stood beside her. "I thought we were going back to where we crossed the creek, but we aren't. I don't know where we are." She shivered. "I don't know what to do now."

"We have to keep going," said Terryl. "We have to get out of the woods sometime."

"That's right," said Pam with a nod.

Sarah sniffed and brushed away tears.

"We could be walking in circles." Dani sounded tired and discouraged.

Pam frowned thoughtfully, then pulled off her hat. "I'll hang this on that branch. If we are going in circles, we'll see my hat and know."

Terryl patted Pam's back. "Good idea!"

Pam puffed up with pride. She usually didn't have the great ideas; Terryl did. "And all along the way we'll leave something."

Sarah giggled. "And we might walk out of the woods with nothing on."

The girls laughed and everyone felt a little better as they started walking again.

"We'll be home before you know it," said Pam brightly. But no one answered her and a shiver trickled down her back.

five
Wild Dogs

Terryl's stomach growled with hunger and she thought about the food that Diane had packed for them in Dani's saddlebags. How she'd love to bite into a cheese sandwich and drink the fruit juice that they'd brought. She sighed and pulled her stomach in until it felt like it touched her backbone. She looked at Dani beside her and back over her shoulder at Pam and Sarah. Were they as hungry as she was?

"Right now I'd like a Big Mac, fries, and a chocolate shake," said Pam, once again reading Terryl's mind. "Or a Wendy's burger and a Frosty!" Her mouth watered thinking about food and her stomach cramped with hunger. Breakfast seemed a long way off. Diane had made them pancakes, sausages, eggs, orange juice (fresh squeezed from sweet oranges), and cold milk. When they lived with Dad they had whatever they fixed themselves. That was usually a bowl of Raisin Bran for herself and a bowl of Wheaties for Terryl. Dad only had a cup of tea and a slice of toast with applebutter smeared over it.

"What's that funny noise?" Sarah stopped walking

and looked around her, gripping the stick tighter. Her sweater and jeans were smeared with mud and a streak of dirt ran from the edge of her eye down to her jaw.

Dani cocked her head and listened. Wind blew through the treetops, but another sound mixed with it. "It sounds almost like a dog panting," she said as her stomach tightened in fear.

"What kind of dog?" Sarah asked. She held her stick like a weapon and shivered.

Pam looked toward a bush and froze. Green eyes were staring back at her! It was a giant tan dog, lying on its haunches, panting as if it had been running hard. Pam couldn't move or speak.

Terryl felt Pam's fear and turned her head and her heart jumped to her throat. "A dog," she whispered, pointing with a trembling hand. She turned her eyes and saw another huge tan dog. Fear pricked her skin and her mouth felt as dry as a bone.

Sarah screamed and the dogs growled.

Dani grabbed Sarah's arm and shushed her. "It must be the wild dogs," she whispered.

Terryl reached for Pam's icy hand and they stood together, shivering with terror. "I'll take care of you, Pam," she said shakily.

Pam squeezed Terryl's hand. With Terryl and the angels and her heavenly Father watching over her, she'd be all right. She turned away from the one dog only to see another one, and then another one. "There are . . . are five . . . five dogs!" she gasped.

"I'm going to faint," moaned Sarah.

"Don't you dare!" Dani gripped Sarah's arm. "I mean it!"

The dogs lined up along one side of the girls, all panting and watching through green slitted eyes. They looked exactly alike—and they all had long sharp teeth that seemed to grow longer and sharper as Terryl watched. Suddenly she couldn't stay still.

"Let's go!" she shouted and took off running, pulling Pam with her.

Dani hesitated, then followed with Sarah, running as fast as she could.

Behind them the dogs barked, filling the air with their howls. Twigs snapped under their giant paws as they ran after the girls, with two dogs on either side of the girls and one following. The barking grew louder and louder and shut off any other sound.

Pain stabbed Pam's side and she clutched at it, but kept running. Branches caught at Terryl's arms and face, scratching her painfully. How she wished Malcom were here with her! He'd face those dogs and fight them off. After this (if there ever was an after this), she'd take Malcom with her everywhere she went. Her monstrous Old English sheepdog would frighten off anything or anybody.

"Jesus, help us," gasped Dani.

Pam's ears rang with the thunderous barking and every muscle in her body ached from running. Suddenly Sarah stumbled and crashed headlong to the ground, pulling Dani with her. Sarah lay facedown on the ground, sprawled out, gasping and whimpering.

Terryl heard the crash and looked back in time to see Dani leap to her feet and bravely face the dog that stopped just inches from her. Terryl spun Pam around and they raced to Dani and stood with her.

Circling the girls, the dogs began, one by one, to lie down, their tongues lolling and their green eyes watching for any movement from the girls.

Time seemed to stand still as the twins and Dani stood back to back and Sarah lay on the ground gasping and sobbing. Suddenly the dogs pricked up their pointed ears, stood up, and loped away together, disappearing into the trees.

Pam sank weakly to the ground and slowly Terryl and Dani followed. No one spoke. Once again wind whistled through the treetops and birds flew from tree to tree. The sun slipped from behind the clouds and lit a path through the woods.

Finally Sarah pushed herself up and looked carefully around. "Where did they go?" she whispered.

No one answered her.

She sat with her legs out in front of her and rubbed her ankle, all the time watching, waiting for the dogs to return. "They didn't eat us, or bite us. How come?"

Still the girls didn't speak.

Sarah pulled up her pant leg, and pushed down her white sock, and studied her ankle. "I think it's broken," she said, and waited for the girls to comment; but they didn't. "Maybe it's just swollen. I guess I can walk on it."

After a long time Dani said, "I guess we'd better . . . go."

"Go . . . where?" asked Terryl.

"Away from here," said Pam, shivering. "Away from the woods." She couldn't say anything about the dogs.

Dani pushed herself up and brushed off the seat of her pants. "Ready?"

Terryl stood up. Her legs felt like water, but she forced herself to walk around until they felt steady again. She wanted to go home and have Mom give her a big hug. Maybe she'd even let David hug her if he wanted; right now she could use all the hugs she could get.

Pam pushed her tangled hair back over her thin shoulders and took a deep breath. "I'm ready. Get up, Sarah, and let's go."

"I think my ankle's broken," Sarah said again.

Pam frowned. "Oh, Sarah!"

"Honest! Look at it." She held up her pant leg. "See?"

"If it was broken you'd be screaming your head off," said Dani impatiently. "Now, stand up and let's go."

Terryl turned away from Sarah's struggle just in time to see a flash of red near a bush. Her eyes widened and she froze apprehensively. As she watched a face appeared around the bush. It was a boy a little older than she, with unruly dark hair and wide gray eyes. "Hey!" she said, starting forward. "Hey, come help us!" He ducked out of sight and she raced toward the bush he'd hidden behind. But when she reached it, he was gone. She stamped the ground, then turned to find the girls right behind her. "Did you see him?"

"Who?" asked Dani, looking around.

Pam frowned. This had better not be another one of Terryl's wild flights of imagination!

Terryl took a deep breath. "I saw a boy standing

right here looking at us! I did! And he had on a red jacket!"

"So?"

"Don't you remember, Dani? We saw someone wearing a red jacket in the woods when we were in the clearing near our . . . your place." She wasn't ready yet to acknowledge that the Big Key was her home as much as it was Dani's. "Remember? The trespasser."

"And you saw him just now?" Dani shivered. "It was a boy?"

"With dark hair and gray eyes. He was a little older than us and he needed a haircut." Terryl faced the woods where he'd run, and cupped her hands around her mouth. "Hey, boy! Come help us! We're lost! Can you hear me? Boy!"

"Are you sure you saw him?" asked Pam.

Terryl scowled at her twin. "I wouldn't make it up, would I?"

"I guess not." Pam rubbed her hands over the jacket sleeves tied at her narrow waist. "Shouldn't we try to find him?"

"Maybe he's lost, too," said Sarah.

Dani stood beside Terryl and shouted, "My name is Danielle Keyes and I live at the Big Key Ranch! We need help! We are lost!" Her voice echoed through the trees, then died away. She sighed and shook her head. "Even if he heard me he's not going to come help. I wonder who it is." She lifted her voice again. "I won't tell my dad you were trespassing! We won't tell anyone that we saw you! Just show us how to get out of here!"

"Dumb boy," muttered Sarah. "I hate him."

"Let's forget about him and keep going," said Terryl. Scalding tears stung her eyes, but she wouldn't let them fall.

"We didn't get to the spot where I left my hat, so we must not be going in circles," said Pam, trying her best to sound cheerful.

"I'll leave my hat here," said Dani. She hung it high on the branch of an oak tree and left it dangling. "Come on, girls. We're going home."

six
The Trespasser

Terryl's steps slowed and she wondered if all the energy had drained from her body. Or maybe she was at home with Dad and asleep in her twin bed, having a terrible nightmare. Maybe Dad would walk in and wake her and tell her that she'd been dreaming, then they'd talk about the book he was writing and how well it would sell.

All of his detective stories sold well enough to provide him a plush apartment with a maid to clean it, a silver sports car, and all the beautiful clothes he wanted. Terryl rubbed her hands down her jeans. Dad liked to dress them in fancy clothes and Mom had always preferred jeans. Mom liked living in the country and Dad liked living in the city. Mom had said that Dad expected too much of her and Dad said that Mom wouldn't grow with him. When he'd finally asked for a divorce, none of them could change his mind. Now, he had a girlfriend named Briana who was a fashion model and Mom was married to David Keyes. But everyone was happy now.

Terryl blinked away a tear. She had tried so hard to get Mom and Dad back together, but nothing had worked. Finally she'd given up, but she still couldn't get used to living in two places. She knew Pam didn't like it either, but she had adjusted better and more quickly than Terryl.

What would Dad say if he knew his daughters were lost in the woods? Maybe he'd try to stop Mom from having them at all. Terryl shuddered and decided that she'd never tell Dad about today.

Pam looked at Terryl and knew she was thinking about their dad. Pam loved her dad, too, but he couldn't understand why she didn't want to play the violin like Terryl. Dad wanted her to do something musical, but being musical didn't interest her. She did like to dress up in the clothes Dad bought her and that pleased him. Terryl preferred wearing jeans and sloppy sweatshirts.

Terryl looked over at Pam and they burst out laughing. "We sure can't tell Dad about today," Terryl said.

"Why not?" asked Dani. She could tell her dad anything.

Terryl shrugged and Pam couldn't find the words to explain.

"I can't tell my dad about today," said Sarah, looking scared again. "He'll be real mad if I'm not home by supper time. Real mad. Will we be home by supper time?"

"I don't know," said Dani with a sigh. "If we can get to a road and follow it to a farmhouse, we could phone home and have someone pick us up."

"I should've stayed home," said Sarah.

"That's for sure!" cried Terryl.

"It's too late to think of that now," said Pam. She

43

stepped over a fallen log. Her legs ached as if she'd just finished two hours of aerobics. She turned to Dani. "Don't you have any idea where we are?"

"I wish I did!"

"So do I," said Terryl in a low, tight voice.

"I want to rest," said Sarah. "My ankle's broken."

Terryl rolled her eyes. "Cut it out, Sarah."

"I mean it! It's broken!"

"You couldn't walk on it if it was," snapped Dani.

"Well, it's gonna be your fault if the doctor has to amputate it! I will have to go through life with one foot. How will that look? Everybody will point at me and say, 'There goes Sarah James with one foot.' And I'll tell them it was all your fault."

"I wish we'd come to a Gingerbread house like in Hansel and Gretel," said Pam with a loud, long sigh. "I'd eat all of it."

"What about the witch inside?" Terryl walked backward so she could see Pam as she walked. "Would you like to have her lock you in a cage and fatten you up?"

"I wouldn't let her catch me. I know the story and I'd know what to watch out for."

"We'd let her have Sarah." Terryl laughed and almost fell down. She turned back around to watch where she was going, then she stopped dead still and Pam ran into her. "Look!" she said, pointing.

The boy in the red jacket stood just ahead of them with his feet apart and his hands on his hips. He wore faded and torn jeans, worn tennis shoes, and the red jacket over a black tee shirt. He brushed his shaggy hair out of his eyes. "You're trespassing! Turn around and go back where you came from!"

Dani's blue eyes widened. "Wes Bremer! It's you! Why didn't you come help us when we called for help?"

"Do you know him?" asked the twins in one voice.

"I've seen him in school." Dani stepped forward with determination. "We will not go back into the swamp!"

Wes narrowed his gray eyes. "Oh, yes, you will! You're trespassing on Bremer property now!"

"Just tell us how to get to the road and we'll leave," said Terryl.

He turned his eyes on her, then on Pam. "Twins, huh? I never saw twins before."

"I'm Terryl and she's Pam. Our mom married Dani's dad and we live on the Big Key."

"So?"

"So nothing! How do we get back to the ranch?" Terryl wanted to leap on him and force out the information they needed.

"You live with your grandma, don't you?" Sarah wagged her finger at Wes.

"What's it to you?"

"My dad knows your grandma. He says she's strange."

Terryl glared at Sarah and Sarah dropped her hand to her side and snapped her mouth closed. "Does your grandma have a phone we can use?" Pam asked. "We have to call our mom."

"It doesn't matter if she does or not, 'cause you aren't going past me!" Wes folded his arms over his chest and set his jaw stubbornly. Streaks of dirt covered his face and twigs hung from his tangled hair.

Terryl looked at Pam and they both looked at Dani, then with a shout they ran at Wes and knocked him to the ground with a thud. Terryl held down his left hand, Pam his right, and Dani sat on his feet. Sarah dropped down beside him and held on to his jacket tail. He struggled and muttered angrily, then finally lay still.

"Tell us what we want to know," said Terryl impatiently.

"You'd better let me go or the swamp monster will get you!" he said.

Sarah shrieked and jumped away from Wes.

"There is no swamp monster," said Dani and the twins agreed.

Wes narrowed his eyes. "I saw it, and I heard it. I can call it anytime I want and it'll come help me." He opened his mouth wide, but before he could shout Terryl clamped her hand over it. He moved his head back and forth and tried to talk.

"Tell us how to get to a phone or we'll keep you here the rest of the day." Terryl leaned down close to him. "We know ways to make you talk," she said dramatically. "So you'd better start now or you'll be very sorry."

He stopped struggling and finally nodded. Slowly she took off her hand, ready to clamp it back on his mouth if he started to yell.

"Let me up and I'll take you to Grandma's. She's really my great-grandma."

The girls released him and stood and watched as

he rubbed his shoulders and pulled his knees up to his chin.

"Come on!" cried Terryl, reaching down for his arm.

Suddenly he did a backward sommersault, sprang to his feet, and ran into the woods, disappearing as if by magic. His taunting laughter floated back to them.

"Oh, my!" Pam stared at the spot where Wes had been.

"He's gone!" Sarah said nervously.

"I'll get him," muttered Dani through her teeth.

Terryl stood speechlessly looking after Wes. One minute he'd been there, and the next he was gone. Maybe he had gone to join his swamp monster. A shiver ran up and down her spine and she swallowed hard.

SEVEN
Discovery

Dani ran forward, but Terryl stopped her with a shout. She turned, frowning, and a sunbeam turned her blonde curls to a bright halo. "Why'd you stop me?" she asked.

"He wants us to follow him, so he can lead us back into the woods where we were." Terryl tucked her honey-brown hair behind her ears. "I think we should look around here and see why he didn't want us to go any further."

"Maybe his house is close by," said Pam excitedly.

"I'd better get home before supper time," muttered Sarah.

Terryl walked forward with the girls behind her, hoping she wasn't going right back into the deep forest again. Then, in the distance, she heard a car horn and she stopped and faced the others with a shout of laughter. "Did you hear that? We *are* getting close to civilization!"

"Just so we're home by supper time," Sarah muttered again.

"There has to be a road or a farm or something!" cried Dani. "Once I see a road I might know where we are."

Several minutes later the trees thinned out. A white-tailed deer crashed through the woods and bounded out of sight.

"Look!" cried Pam, pointing ahead.

"A dirt road!" shouted Dani, running full tilt toward it with the other close behind and beside her. She stopped in the middle of the road and twirled around and around with her arms wide.

Terryl raced up the dirt road, turned and raced back, shouting and laughing and blinking back tears.

Pam stood quietly and let warm tears slip down her flushed cheeks. Soon she'd be home, safe in Mom's arms. She'd walk into her beautiful bedroom that Mom had decorated for her in shades of purple, her favorite color. She sniffed and wiped away her tears, ready to go as soon as Dani and Terryl stopped being so dramatic.

Sarah twisted her toe in the dirt in the middle of the road as she watched Dani and Terryl. "When are we going home?"

"Right now!" shouted Terryl, leaping high.

"Look at this!" cried Dani, looking down at the dirt road. "Pony tracks. Lots of pony tracks. They could be our ponies! Let's follow them." Her eyes sparkled and she laughed. "We might not have to call home."

Pam's stomach tightened. No way would she get on a pony and ride home; she'd rather walk! But she didn't say anything. She just walked along with the others, following Dani as she tracked the hoofprints and an occasional pile of manure.

"My ankle hurts," Sarah said, bending down to rub it. But no one stopped and she ran after them,

49

tugging her blue sweater down over her jeans as she ran.

Soon the ponies' tracks turned off the dirt road onto a narrow lane. Dani didn't hesitate, but ran along the tree-lined lane.

Terryl wanted to call her back to the road so they could follow it to a highway, but she knew Dani wouldn't listen to her. It was hard to get used to having a new sister, especially one like Dani. Dani was used to having her own way, but she wasn't spoiled. She was better at more things than Terryl, except for violin. Dani didn't want to play violin, but her Uncle Mark—David's brother—played. Terryl enjoyed listening to him play and talk. He'd told her that if she kept practicing she could someday play in the symphony if she wanted. Maybe Mark would be at the ranch when they returned.

Suddenly Dani turned and pressed her finger to her lips for silence. She ducked behind a clump of bushes with tiny green leaves and motioned for the others to follow her. She waited until the others crouched down beside her. "There's a farm just ahead. I saw the buildings through the trees. It might be the Bremer place and if it is we don't want to run into Wes and have him stop us."

"We don't want to run into Granny Bremer," whispered Sarah. "Dad says she carries a shotgun around with her and will shoot trespassers on sight." She moved closer to Dani.

"Is that true?" asked Pam, frowning. She had no intention of walking anywhere that she'd be shot.

"That's only a rumor," said Dani. "People say my Gran wears a six-gun on her hip just like Calamity

Jane in the old West just because she dresses like a cowboy and trains horses. And you know Gran doesn't carry a gun."

"Does Gran know Mrs. Bremer?" asked Terryl, peering through the bushes. All she could see was the corner of a weathered barn.

"Gran knows her. She said Mrs. Bremer and Great-grandma Morgan once were best friends." Dani rubbed her nose with the back of her hand. "I've seen Mrs. Bremer in town a couple of times, but I've never talked to her. She wouldn't know me at all."

"Well, we can't stay behind this bush all day," said Pam.

Dani bit her bottom lip. "I'm going to sneak up to the barn and see if our ponies are inside. If they are, I'll bring them out and we'll ride out of here for home."

Pam locked her icy hands together and forced back a shudder.

"I'll go with you," said Terryl.

Pam's eyes grew big and round. "Oh, Terryl!"

"I'll be all right. I will. Won't I, Dani?"

"As long as you keep quiet and follow me." Dani stood and pressed her hands to the small of her back. "If the ponies are inside the barn we might have to saddle them. Are you sure you can do that, Terryl?"

"Gran taught me how."

"Let's go, then."

Sarah plucked at Dani's sleeve. "Don't you dare get shot or I won't make it home by supper time."

Dani frowned and brushed Sarah's pudgy hand

away. "If we aren't back in a short time, come find us. But be careful!"

Pam shivered. Maybe it would be easier to go with Terryl and Dani instead of staying behind waiting for them. Sweat popped out on her forehead and she wiped it off with the back of her hand.

Terryl followed Dani, creeping behind trees and bushes to the side of the wooden fence near the barn. A mule stood inside the pen chomping on a mouthful of hay, its long ears flicking back and forth. It ignored the girls and Terryl was glad.

Just then, a dog barked and Terryl grabbed Dani's arm. Dani pulled free and crept along the fence to the large barn door that was closed and latched shut with a heavy board. Dani looked around, then lifted the board and pushed it back. The door swung open and she dodged inside. Terryl followed her, and Dani pulled the door closed.

"It's dark in here," whispered Terryl. She heard rustling noises and hoped a mouse wouldn't run up her pant leg.

"Follow me." Dani crept forward with Terryl close behind. The barn smelled like old hay and fresh manure. A horse nickered and Dani stopped. "Lizzy? Is that you, Lizzy?"

A horse nickered again and bumped against the stall. Dani ran to a closed stall and peered over the door. A long-eared donkey lifted its head and brayed. Terryl jumped back, then giggled self-consciously. Dani ran to the next stall and looked inside.

"Lizzy!" Dani reached over the door and touched Lizzy's soft nose. "I am so happy to see you!"

Terryl patted the pony's spotted neck, then patted the other two as they pushed up to the door. None of them wore saddles or bridles.

Dani looked around, her eyes growing accustomed to the dimness. "I wonder where the tack is." She ran down the aisle toward the back of the barn where bales of hay were stacked. A cat zipped out of her way, leaped up on a bale, and hissed with its back arched and tail fluffed to twice its size.

Terryl ran to another stall and looked inside. It was empty. She checked the next stall to find a small calf curled in a pile of straw.

The barn door creaked and Terryl and Dani leaped for cover, Dani behind a bale of hay and Terryl inside the empty stall. Her heart hammered so loud she was sure Dani could hear it at the other end of the barn.

"Are you in here, Terryl?"

It was Pam, and Terryl sagged in relief, then jumped out and hauled Pam inside. Sarah followed, shaking with fright.

"Why did you girls come?" asked Dani.

"We saw Wes again and we were afraid he'd find you in here," said Pam, hooking her hair behind her ears. "We came to warn you."

"We found the ponies," said Terryl. "But we can't find the saddles."

Suddenly the barn door swung wide and bright sunlight streamed in, blinding the girls. They stood in the dirt aisle and stared at the black form that blocked out a section of the sunlight.

"You're trespassing!"

It was Wes, and Terryl stepped forward, her fists doubled at her sides.

"Get out of here before I call Granny!" Wes said, motioning for them to come out. Finally, one by one, they walked out of the barn to stand in the trampled yard.

"We won't leave without our ponies!" Dani stuck out her chin and crossed her thin arms over her thin chest.

"What ponies?" asked Wes.

"The ones inside," said Terryl. "There are three of them, and they belong to us."

Wes narrowed his eyes. "Wanna bet? They're in our barn on our property. That makes 'em ours."

EIGHT
Trouble with Wes

Pam stared at Wes with her mouth open in surprise. How could he think that he could keep the ponies just because they were in his barn? She looked at Dani to see how she was taking Wes's announcement. By the angry sparks shooting from her eyes Pam knew she wouldn't accept what Wes had said.

"Terryl, get the ponies," said Dani.

"Don't try it, Terryl." Wes stepped forward menacingly. "If you even take one step into that barn, I'll sic the dogs on you."

"Dogs?" Sarah looked around, trembling with fear.

"What dogs?" asked Dani. "Do you have imaginary dogs all around you, Wes Bremer? First you think my ponies are yours and then you think you're going to sic imaginary dogs on us." She laughed, but it sounded shaky.

Terryl measured the distance between herself and Wes. If he did have dogs close at hand, maybe she could reach him before he could call or whistle to them. She tensed, ready to spring, watching him and waiting for the perfect moment.

Dani's teasing voice continued and Wes's face

turned bright red as he glared at her. Suddenly Terryl lunged forward, catching Wes by surprise and knocking him to the ground. He was at least a head taller than she was and much heavier. But before he could throw her off, the others leaped on him, pinning him to the ground. Terryl clamped her hands over his mouth as she straddled his chest.

"Drag him inside the barn before his grandma sees us," said Dani.

Together they pulled and puffed and managed to get him inside the barn with him fighting them all the way. They pushed him into the empty stall and locked the door, then peered over it at him where he lay in the dirty straw.

He leaped up, his eyes flashing, and stood with his feet apart, his fists doubled at his sides, his chin thrust out. "You'll be sorry for doing this to me!"

"Tell us where the saddles and bridles are and we'll leave," said Dani in a voice that she'd learned from her dad, who was used to giving orders and having them followed.

"I'll never tell!" Wes flung his hair out of his eyes. "And when Granny comes to do the chores and finds you here, you'll all be very, very sorry!"

"I'm scared. Real scared," Dani said sarcastically.

"You should be!" Wes lunged at the door and the girls leaped back. The door shook, but didn't open. "Let me out right now!"

"Not before you tell us what we want to know!" Terryl stood with her hands on her narrow waist. "Start talking!"

A cat meowed and the girls jumped. Lizzy

nickered and Dani called to her, telling her that they'd be leaving soon.

Wes flopped down on the stall floor and sat cross-legged with his hands on his knees. "I got all day," he said lazily.

"I'm going to look for the saddles," said Pam. She couldn't stand to see Wes locked up like a wild animal. She didn't like what he was doing to them, but she wanted to set him free and forget about the saddles and the ponies.

She walked up and down the aisle looking for the tack. She climbed the ladder that led to the haymow, but all she saw was a mouse streak out of sight. She bit back a scream and dropped back down to the dirt floor. She heard the others talking to Wes, trying to convince him and threaten him into telling them where they could find the saddles.

She opened the door and eased outside, blinking against the bright sunlight. Cautiously she looked around, then walked toward a run down shed several feet away.

Wind ruffled her hair. Dogs barked and Pam lifted her head, startled, suddenly alert to every sound, every movement. From the sound of the barks she knew it was several dogs. Could the dogs that had chased them in the woods be nearby? She trembled and swallowed hard, then dashed back to the safety of the barn.

"What's wrong?" asked Terryl.

"Dogs," whispered Pam.

"Dogs?" Sarah grabbed Pam's arm and shook it. "Where are they? Can they get in here?"

Wes shook the stall door and they all turned to face him. "I told you I'd sic the dogs on you. Well, I won't have to. Granny will. Big ugly wild dogs that will think you're dinner!" He tipped back his head and laughed. "Wait and see. If they frightened you in the woods, they'll scare you to death now."

The girls looked toward the barn door, then back at Wes. "You're making it all up," said Dani.

"I didn't make up the dogs, and you know it!"

"I want to go home," whispered Sarah. "I don't want to be near the dogs. Let's leave the ponies and go."

The dogs barked again, but now they were just outside the barn. Terryl wanted to grab Wes and shake him. Suddenly the barking stopped and a crackly voice called, "Wes! You find the cow, Wes?"

"I'm in the barn, Granny!" he called out.

Terryl lunged for the stall door to clamp her hand over Wes's mouth, but she was too late. The barn door opened and dogs swarmed in. The girls screamed and the dogs barked and growled.

"Quiet!" yelled Granny. She wore baggy denim overalls with a plaid shirt, the sleeves rolled almost to her elbows. She was short and skinny and looked as though a slap from one of the dogs' tails could easily knock her off her feet. A wide brimmed, greasy hat covered her head. Wisps of gray hair poked out near her gray eyes, which were watching them all closely.

"What's going on in here?" she demanded. "Dogs! I said quiet! You hush when I say hush!" She peered from under her hat brim at the girls and at Wes in the stall. "What's going on here? Speak up! Cat got your tongues? Want I should sic my dogs on you?" She shook a bony finger at them.

"They say the ponies belong to them, Granny."

Terryl nodded, careful not to make a quick move and startle the dogs into attacking her. "The ponies do belong to us. We have to get them and get home."

"But Wes won't tell us where the tack is," said Dani.

Sarah pressed against the rough stall, trembling with such fear that she thought she'd faint. But she was afraid if she fainted, a dog would eat her and she wouldn't even know it.

"Please, Mrs. Bremer, we need your help," said Pam softly.

Granny looped a thumb around her suspender and studied the girls. "I see you girls are strong. Else how would the boy get locked up?"

Wes flushed and ducked his head. "There's four of them!"

"So it seems." Granny pushed her hat to the back of her small, round head. "I see we got us some real trading coming up."

"What do you mean?" asked Dani.

"You want your ponies and your tack, and I want something just as bad. Yes, sir, I sure do." She snapped her fingers and the giant tan dogs pressed against her legs. "Boys, get outside while I work this thing out." She waited until the dogs loped from the barn and lay down just outside the door.

Sarah inched her way toward Pam and reached out for her. Pam smiled weakly and took Sarah's hand and held it tight.

"What's your deal?" asked Terryl. She didn't want to have to trade for their horses, but she didn't want to stand inside the barn for the rest of her life either.

"Don't make no deal with them, Granny." Wes worked with the lock and finally pushed the stall door open. He glared at the girls and walked to Granny's side. "Send them away, Granny. We don't need to make a deal with them."

"Hush, boy!"

He flushed and ducked his head.

"What is the deal?" Terryl repeated impatiently.

Granny rubbed her wrinkled face. "Get off your high horse, girl." She looked closer at Terryl and Pam. "Twins. I'll be switched! Twin girls. Jest like two peas in a pod." She chuckled and Terryl's anger rose.

Pam reached over and squeezed Terryl's arm to tell her not to get angry. Terryl forced back her sharp words and waited.

"I am Danielle Keyes and the twins are my sisters, Terryl and Pamela Tyler. And that's Sarah James, our neighbor."

Granny slapped her leg and dust flew. "I won't remember your names two seconds after you tell me. But that won't matter. I got this here deal figured out in my head, and here's what it is. You girls want your ponies and your tack. I want my . . . I want my house cleaned!"

"Granny!" Wes stared at her as if she'd lost her mind.

The girls looked at each other. None of them had had much experience in cleaning a house, but if that's what it took to get their ponies and be on their way, then they'd do it. Terryl cocked an eyebrow and studied Granny Bremer thoughtfully. Something was up, something more than just cleaning a house. But what was it?

"Follow me." Granny turned and walked out of the barn. "Wes, you shut the door behind us." The dogs jumped and waited for orders from Granny with their ears pricked up, their bodies still. She made a motion with her hand and the dogs fell in behind the girls and they all walked across the yard toward the small gray farmhouse that looked to be older than Granny.

Terryl glanced over her shoulder to find the dogs on her heels. Even if she wanted to run, she'd never get away from those dogs. She'd have to pretend to go along with anything Granny said, then grab the first chance she could to get away. She frowned as she realized that even if she managed to get away she wouldn't know how to get back to the Big Key for help. Her heart sank. There was nothing she could do, nothing at all.

NiNE
Granny Bremer's Deal

Granny led the girls to the kitchen. The dogs lay just outside the kitchen door, watching and waiting. Granny had shown the girls through two bedrooms, a living room, a bathroom, and now the kitchen. The rooms were cluttered but not really dirty, which made Terryl even more suspicious.

"You girls eat any lunch today?" Granny leaned against the counter near the sink and looked at the girls lined up by a small round table.

"No," said Dani, and the others echoed the word.

"You'll work better on full stomachs." Granny took a jar of peanut butter out of the cupboard. "There's milk in the icebox and bread right here. Make yourselves peanut butter and jelly sandwiches."

"We don't want your food," said Terryl stiffly, but her stomach cried out for food of any kind. She stuffed her hands in her pockets to keep from grabbing the jar of peanut butter and a spoon and wolfing down the creamy contents.

"Don't listen to her," said Sarah. "We're hungry."

"We have to eat, Terryl," whispered Pam, her face white and strained.

"We'll eat," said Dani with a firm nod. "But we won't enjoy it!"

"Don't matter to me." Granny walked to the door, then turned and stood with her gray head tilted, one wrinkled hand wrapped around a suspender and the other one on her skinny hip. "By the way, girls, if you happen to run across an old canvas bag about the size of a tablet of paper bring it to me. It's gray with black lettering on it." She shrugged. "It's not of much importance, but bring it to me anyhow." She pushed open the screen door and it squeaked. Immediately the dogs leaped to their feet. "I'll feed the boys and be right back inside."

Terryl stood very still, her heart hammering against her rib cage. Not for a second did Terryl believe that the bag wasn't important to Granny; it was probably the real reason Granny needed their help: to find that bag . . . and whatever was in it.

"What're you thinking, Terryl?" whispered Dani as Pam and Sarah washed their hands at the sink so they could make sandwiches.

"About the canvas bag."

Dani frowned and shrugged. "What about it?"

"I think Granny Bremer wants it worse than she's letting on."

"So what?"

Impatiently Terryl hooked her hair over her ears. "So nothing, Dani. How should I know what's happening here?"

"Don't get mad at me!"

Terryl sighed raggedly. "Sorry. It's just that we need a plan and I thought I could think of one. I thought the canvas bag might help, but I don't know how."

"I guess we'd better eat. If we find the bag, we'll see then."

Terryl nodded and walked to the sink to wash her hands. Maybe the canvas bag was no big deal, maybe she was grabbing at anything right now. She'd forget about any great plan and she'd help clean the house, get their ponies and tack, and get out of here.

She choked down a sandwich and a glass of milk while sitting at the table with the girls. Granny was still outdoors with the dogs. Terryl wiped her mouth off with her sleeve, then leaned forward. "Girls, search for that canvas bag." She saw Dani's frown, but she ignored it. "If you find it bring it to me and we'll all decide what to do with it. I think it is very important to Mrs. Bremer. I know I could be wrong, Dani, but that's the way I feel. So, we'll look for it. OK?"

The door squeaked and Granny walked in, frowning. "You still eating? I didn't say you could eat me out of house and home, did I? Now, get your tails moving and get to work!"

Each of the girls had been assigned a room to clean. Granny had said she'd already finished the bathroom, and had assigned Pam to Wes's room, Sarah to the living room, and Dani to the kitchen. Terryl ran to Granny's bedroom.

A large old-fashioned bed filled most of Granny's room. A bookcase full of books stood against the wall near the closet door. A chair and a seven-drawer chest were the only other things in the room. Books were scattered about, as well as a few pieces of clothing. A newspaper was pulled apart and dropped on the carpet.

Terryl peeked in the closet expecting to see rows of clothes like her grandmother in Detroit had and Gran at the Big Key had. But the worn shirts that hung there were more like those Grandad wore to work. Three pairs of bibbed overalls hung on hooks. Far back in the closet a garment bag hung almost out of sight. Terryl opened it to find a yellowed lace wedding gown that Granny had probably worn when she was young. On a shelf, Terryl found an old picture album of a young Granny with a man beside her. He must have been her husband, and the small boys in the picture were her sons.

In the very back of the book was a school photo of Wes. In the picture he had a new haircut and wore a clean shirt. He was very good-looking. Terryl frowned. What was different about Wes? Suddenly it hit her. In the picture he looked just like any other boy without a care in the world; he looked happy. The Wes that was outside right now was not the same happy boy, nor the same clean, well-taken-care-of boy. What had happened?

Terryl shrugged. It was no concern of hers. She was here to get a job done, and she'd do it as quickly as possible.

She stuffed the books back in the bookcase, making sure there was no canvas bag hidden among them. She dropped on all fours and looked under the bed only to find dust balls and a baseball bat. She pulled back the quilt and the blanket and the sheet. She lifted the pillows and hoisted up the mattress. There was no sign of the canvas bag. With a tired sigh she made the bed and dropped the pillows in place. She folded up the newspaper and dropped it on the chair. Quickly she searched the seven-drawer chest, but there was no canvas bag.

She stepped out into the living room to find Sarah struggling with the heavy sofa. The room looked clean, and Terryl was surprised. She didn't think Sarah knew how to do any housework. She'd been inside Sarah's house once and saw how cluttered it was. Sarah didn't seem to mind a mess even though she spent long hours all alone in her house because her parents worked.

Terryl grabbed the sofa and helped Sarah move it. Then Sarah stepped back with a frown.

"I thought I saw something under it," she said. She knelt down and picked up some wadded paper, a pencil, and several bits of colored yarn. "I didn't find the bag."

"Me neither." Terryl helped put the sofa back in place. "Did you check between the cushions?" She'd lost things in her couch at home between cushions.

"I looked, but all I found was a quarter and a pair of scissors." She pointed to them on the end table. She rubbed her hands up and down her arms. "Terryl, are we ever going to get to leave here?"

Terryl stiffened. "What do you mean?"

"What if Granny keeps us prisoners? She'll make us be her slaves."

Terryl shook her head. "She wouldn't dare!"

Sarah relaxed a little. "I hope you're right." She looked around with a strange expression on her face. "I guess I'll go help Dani in the kitchen. I want to go home."

Terryl watched Sarah walk way, then she went to Wes's room to help Pam. Pam sat huddled in the corner of the room with her hands over her face. "Pam, what's wrong?" Terryl dropped beside her and tugged at her hands.

Pam sniffed and blinked back tears. "I cleaned the room and I searched everywhere, but I couldn't find the canvas bag! What if we can't find it at all? What will Mrs. Bremer do to us if we don't find the bag?"

"Probably nothing, Pam. I bet I was wrong about it being important. I bet she did only want us to clean her house." Terryl forced a smile. "I bet we'll be on our way home in just a few minutes."

Pam shook her head. "Don't, Terryl. You're not making me feel better. I know that's what you're trying to do. I'm not a baby, you know." Pam pushed herself up and flipped back her hair. "I just want to go home!"

"Me, too, Pammie. Me, too. Let's go see if Dani found anything."

In the kitchen, Dani sat with her elbows on the table and her chin in her hands. Sarah stood near the sink drinking a glass of water.

"Did you find it?" Terryl asked at the same time Dani did. They both stopped, then asked again, then they both shook their heads.

"Who's going to tell Mrs. Bremer?" asked Pam.

"We won't say anything unless she asks," said Terryl. "Let me do the talking." She turned to Sarah. "Understand?"

"Why're you looking at me?"

"Just don't say anything about the bag."

"I won't." Sarah flounced across the room. "Why won't anyone trust me? You'd think I'm the only one in the room that ever causes trouble."

Terryl rolled her eyes, but didn't say anything. "Let's go find Mrs. Bremer." She led the way to the screen door. Hesitantly she pushed it open. Immediately the dogs started barking.

Granny Bremer ran around the house and stopped in front of the door. "All done, girls?"

"The house is clean," said Terryl. She held the door wide for the others, then closed it after herself. A warm breeze blew her hair. "We're ready to go. Tell us where the saddles are and we'll be on our way."

Granny chuckled. "Sure enough."

Pam felt weak all over. They really were going to get to leave!

"Follow me." Granny quieted the dogs and walked across the yard with the girls close behind. She stopped and turned. "By the way, where did you find the canvas bag? Did you leave it on the table for me?"

"What canvas bag?" Terryl sounded very innocent and she widened her dark eyes.

Pam's heart sank. Dani and Sarah stood very still, waiting.

Granny frowned. "No matter."

"Did you need the bag?" asked Terryl.

"Not particularly." Granny cleared her throat. "You're sure you didn't run across it?"

Terryl lifted her shoulders and let them fall.

"No matter," Granny said again, but her voice sounded strained. She turned and started walking. The girls followed. Granny stopped again and pulled off her hat and scratched her head. "This mind sure don't work like it once did. I can't recall where I put them saddles."

The girls cried out and Terryl quieted them with a look.

"What will make you remember?" asked Terryl in a tense voice.

Granny put her hat back on her head. The dogs lay at her feet, watching and waiting. "I'll have to give it some more thought. While I'm thinking, you girls can go stack the pile of wood up against the side of the house."

"No!" cried Dani.

Terryl took a deep breath. "Will you remember where the saddles are once the wood is stacked or will you find other jobs for us to do?"

Granny poked out her bottom lip in a pout. "You hurt me, girl, hurt me deep. We got us a deal. You do what I ask and I'll let you go home with them ponies." She walked them to the woodpile and showed them how to stack the wood. She stepped back and narrowed her eyes. "It could be you'll run across that gray canvas bag of mine in that woodpile. Tell me if you do."

Terryl shot a knowing look at the girls, but didn't speak until Granny and the dogs disappeared inside a small shed several yards away. "That bag must be very important to Mrs. Bremer," she said when she

69

figured it was safe. "She lost it, or she thinks somebody took it, but I don't think she'll let us go until we find it."

"What if we never find it?" whispered Sarah, her eyes wide and watery.

The twins and Dani looked at each other without speaking, then slowly turned and started stacking the wood in a pile.

TEN
Terryl's Find

Terryl's back ached, her arms ached, and her hands
ached. Every muscle in her body was sore from
stacking wood, and there was still more to be done.
Worst of all, there was no sign of the gray canvas
bag.

"I can't pick up another piece," said Pam, looking
at her red and scratched palms. "I think I have a
sliver in my thumb." She looked closer, then Terryl
took her hand and looked.

"I see it." Terryl picked at the end of the splinter,
finally caught hold of it and pulled it out. Pam
popped her finger into her mouth with a groan. "I
think we should just grab the ponies and ride out of
here and send David back for the saddles," Terryl
muttered.

Pam clutched Terryl's arm before she could run to
tell Dani her idea. "I can't ride, Terryl! Not ever!"

"What do you mean?"

Pam flushed to the roots of her hair. "I know
you'll think I'm just a big scared baby, but I don't
care! I will never, ever ride another horse! I mean it,
Terryl! When we leave here, I'll walk and let Sarah
ride my pony."

Terryl could tell that Pam was serious, and when her sister made up her mind she could be very stubborn. "I won't make you ride, Pam. I just didn't know you were that scared."

"Well, I am."

Terryl nodded. "Let's just get Dani and get out of here." But when they turned they saw Granny and the dogs standing across the yard watching them. Terryl's heart sank. "I guess we'd better get back to work."

With a ragged sigh Pam walked to the woodpile beside Sarah and picked up a chunk of split wood.

Terryl narrowed her eyes as she watched Granny. The minute Granny turned to talk to the dogs, Terryl slipped around the corner of the house, then dashed for cover behind a lilac bush. Shivers of fear ran up and down her spine. She would find the saddles on her own and then they would leave, no matter what Granny said or did. Terryl thought of the dogs and her courage almost failed, but she lifted her chin high and squared her shoulders. Somehow they had to get away.

Cautiously she looked around. She'd already been inside the barn and the house. There were still the garage and two sheds to search. Once she found the saddles and bridles she planned to carry them to the barn, and get the ponies ready to go. Then she'd ride to the woodpile, rescue the girls, and they'd all ride like the wind for the ranch.

She smiled at the picture in her mind; she'd be a heroine for sure. But then she remembered that Pam had said she'd never ride a horse again. How would she get Pam home if she wouldn't ride?

"I won't think about that," she muttered. "I'll just think about finding the saddles."

She ran to the nearest shed and dodged around the end of it, so that she was out of sight of the house. Her chest rose and fell and she swallowed hard to relieve the dryness in her mouth. Slowly she crept around the shed to the door, eased it open, and slipped inside. Old machinery stood on the dirt floor, and cobwebs hung along the rafters and over the windows. There were no saddles in sight and no place to tuck them away out of sight. Her heart sank and for a second tears burned her eyes. She blinked and swallowed hard. She did not have time to cry or to feel sorry for herself.

Carefully she opened the door a crack and peered out. When she saw the coast was clear, she slipped out and ran for a tree near the other shed.

A dog barked and Granny quieted it. From the barn a pony whinnied. Terryl crouched near the tree trunk, her heart thudding so loud she was afraid Granny would hear it and sic the dogs on her.

Slowly she peeked around the tree, then dashed to the shed and slipped inside. Her eyes widened and her heart leaped—the saddles were there, set on three sawhorses, and the bridles hung from hooks on the center post of the shed. She ran to them and touched them, feeling the smooth leather of the saddles and the prickly wool of the blankets. She leaned her cheek against the bridles and felt the hard leather and cool steel.

Could she get the things to the barn without being seen?

Butterflies fluttered in her stomach. Dare she even

73

try to get them to the barn? A spider dangled down near her face and she jumped, forcing back a scream.

Just then the shed door burst open and Wes jumped inside. Terryl fell back against a saddle, her eyes wide with alarm.

"I thought I'd find you here, Terryl!"

"Don't touch me! I mean it!"

He stopped just inches from her, glaring at her. "I wouldn't want to touch you unless it would be to punch your lights out for what you did to me before."

She held out her hands, palms up. "All we wanted to do was get our ponies and go home. We didn't want to hurt you, or embarrass you."

He pushed back his hair. "I know that, I guess."

"We want to go home. I'm afraid your granny will keep us here until we find the canvas bag."

Wes jerked back. "What do you know about the canvas bag?"

"Only that your granny wants it real bad."

"Did she say so?"

Terryl shook her head. "She didn't have to. I could tell. What's in it that's so important anyway?"

He doubled his fists and growled deep in his throat. "I hate that gray canvas bag!"

Terryl stepped forward, suddenly intrigued. "Why?"

"I shouldn't tell you."

"Sure you should. Maybe I can help."

He sighed and brushed his hair back again. "Granny's money is in it, and she lost it." He groaned and shook his head. "She was afraid I was going to take it and run away from home."

"And were you?"

"I tried once, but she caught me." His face turned red. "I promised I wouldn't do it again, and I meant it. But she doesn't believe me. I told her I was mad and that's why I was going to leave and take her money." He moved restlessly. "So, every day since then she's been putting the canvas bag in a new location. But she hid it two weeks ago and she hasn't been able to find it. Her memory's not what it used to be. I think she hid it in the trash and burned it, but she won't listen to me. Sometimes she thinks I have it, but I don't!"

"Have you tried to find it?"

He nodded.

"We didn't see it in the house," Terryl said. "I hope she didn't burn it."

"So do I. Its all the savings she has. She had it in the bank and then she got a crazy notion that it wasn't safe there, so she took it all out." Wes walked back and forth near the door. "I wanted your ponies so I could sell them and show the money to Granny and tell her it was her savings. But I know now that won't work; you girls wouldn't let me do that."

"No, we wouldn't!"

Wes hoisted a saddle to his shoulder. "Come on . . . I'll help you get your ponies ready so you can go home. Granny shouldn't try to keep you here any longer. She'll be in big trouble with your family and the police. I don't want that to happen." He stopped at the door and looked back at Terryl. "Grab a saddle. I'll tell you when it's safe to go."

She lifted a saddle and tried to carry it the way he

75

was, but it was too heavy and she stumbled and almost fell.

"I guess you'd better carry the saddle blankets," he said with a sigh. "I'll have to make several trips back and forth."

Terryl gathered up the three blankets and followed Wes. But before they could go anywhere Granny and her dogs blocked the door.

"Stabbed in the back by my own flesh and blood!" Granny pulled off her hat and held it to her breast. "How can I survive this much pain?"

Terryl backed away and dropped the blankets.

Wes flushed, but he looked Granny in the eye. "We can't keep them here, and you know it. They've got families and they have to get home. I'll help you look for your bag. You don't need these girls."

"Since when are you the boss around here, boy?" Granny clamped her hat back on her head. "Did you find the cow?"

"No."

"Then get out there and look for her! She could be caught in the swamp."

"With the swamp monster?" asked Terryl.

"Swamp monster?" Granny chuckled and shook her head. "No such a thing, girlie. Just something folks made up to keep other folks away." She turned back to Wes. "Put the saddle back and get out after that cow!"

"I'll go, Granny, but first you let these girls go home before their families call the police."

"Don't tell me what to do, Wesley Bremer! Now, get!"

His face darkened and his jaw set stubbornly. "I won't do it! I won't leave here until the girls are gone. I mean it, Granny!" He flung the saddle back over the sawhorse, then marched right past Granny and across the yard to the woodpile where he started stacking wood with the others.

"I never!" Granny pressed her lips tightly together. "That boy is too much of a handful. An old lady shouldn't be raising such a young boy."

"He told me about your bag of money," Terryl said softly.

Granny fell back a step. "He did what?"

"We'll try to find it for you, but we can't stay much longer."

Granny shook her head and sighed heavily. "It's getting so you can't trust nobody! My own flesh and blood is telling my secrets!"

"It doesn't matter. We won't tell anyone. At least, we won't tell anyone if you let us go right now. That's *our* deal!"

Granny rubbed a wrinkled hand across her overalls. "Things are getting out of hand. Maybe Wes is right. Maybe I should let you go."

Terryl's heart leaped. She ducked her head to hide her excitement from Granny. If she appeared too eager Granny might change her mind.

"I'm too old for all this flurry." Granny turned to her dogs. "Boys, get to the house and wait for me there."

The dogs padded to the house and dropped to the ground near the back door.

Terryl peeked through her dark lashes at Granny.

Granny suddenly did look very old and very tired. Pity for her stirred inside Terryl, surprising her. "I'm sorry you can't find your money."

Granny's gray eyes sparked. "Don't you say no more about that money of mine! That's my business and mine alone!"

Terryl flushed and snapped her mouth closed.

"Get over there with the others. What're you waiting on? Get!" Granny waved her hat at Terryl. "Don't just stand there, girl! You got lead in your feet?"

Terryl lifted her chin and squared her shoulders. "We will stay one more hour to help you find your money, and then we're going home!"

"You don't say?"

"You know you don't want trouble with our families or with the police. And you sure don't want the world to know that you keep your money here at your house in a canvas bag that anyone could steal." Terryl narrowed her dark eyes. "Do we have a deal?"

Granny turned her head and shouted, "Boys! Come!"

The dogs leaped up, barking with a vengeance, and ran at top speed to Granny's side.

Terryl shrank back, the color draining from her face, and Granny looked at her with a smug smile.

"What do you say now, smart girl?" she asked.

Terryl hung her head and didn't say anything.

ElEVEN
The Lost Cow

Granny went to the woodpile and gripped Wes's arm. She hauled him away from the girls, and pushed him toward the woods. "I want you out there after that cow right this minute, Wesley Bremer!"

Pam saw the flush spread over Wes's neck and face and it made her feel terrible. "We'll help him find the cow." The words were out before she knew she was going to say them. But now that they were out, she was glad of it, no matter what the others said.

Granny and Wes turned to stare at Pam in surprise and the girls cried, "Pam!"

She lifted her head high and looked right at Granny. "We'll help Wes find the cow."

"Why should you do that?" Granny dropped Wes's arm and stood with her hands on her skinny hips, her eyebrows raised almost to the brim of her hat.

Pam looked helplessly at Terryl, but knew her twin wouldn't help her. Dani might understand because she knew that Jesus wanted them to be kind to others and love them with action and not just words. Finally Pam turned back to Granny and

Wes. "He . . . he told us the cow was missing and he told us how important it is to you."

Dani stepped forward to stand beside Pam. "He said he was out looking for the cow when he saw us. We kept him from doing his job, so we want to help him now."

Granny pulled off her hat and scratched her head. "Well, I'll be switched. I didn't think there were folks around that would help a body in need. What'd you say your name was?"

"Danielle Keyes. My great-grandmother was Danielle Morgan."

Granny frowned thoughtfully and finally nodded. "Sure enough. Sure, you do favor her with them blonde curls. What a small world!"

"I don't need help finding the cow, Granny," Wes said. "Send the girls home so there won't be no trouble." He looked up at his granny with wide pleading eyes. "You don't know how much trouble you'll be in if the girls tell what you did to them today."

"What'd I do? Tell me that!" she demanded.

"You forced us to stay here, that's what!" Sarah pushed her blue sweater sleeves up her rounded arms to her dimpled elbows. "And if I don't get home by supper time my dad'll have a fit!"

"Quiet, Sarah!" Dani scowled at Sarah and Sarah snapped her mouth shut. "We'll help Wes, but we'd better call home first to tell them where we are."

"We don't have a phone," said Wes.

"We still have time to help find the cow," said Pam. "Let us help, Mrs. Bremer. We want to. We feel badly that both your bag of money and your cow are lost."

Terryl held her breath, waiting for Granny to explode. When she didn't Terryl looked closer at her. The old woman seemed to shrink right before her eyes. "Mrs. Bremer, what's wrong? Are you sick?" Terryl leaped forward and caught Granny's thin arm.

Granny blinked fast, but tears still slid down her wrinkled cheeks. "I am an old woman without any secrets. It's too much to take."

"Are you all right, Granny? You look pale." Wes held her other arm. "We'll take you to the house and you can lie down." He shouted for the dogs to stay and together he and Terryl helped Granny to the house where they settled her on the living room sofa. Dani brought her a glass of cold water and she sipped it and handed the rest back.

"I am all right! Stop fussing over me. I'm not used to being fussed over." She ran a shaky hand through her gray hair. "I guess it's pretty hard on me to have my money and my cow gone. But it's harder still to have all of you know about it."

"Maybe now you'll put your money back in the bank after we find it," said Wes.

"Mind what you say, boy!" Granny sighed, then grinned. "You're right, Wes. I guess it would be better to put that money in the bank."

"Or you could buy a safe and have it installed in here," said Pam. "Grandmother in Detroit did that. She said it made her feel better."

"That's a good idea," Granny said. "I could do that."

"So long as you didn't lose the combination," said Wes with a laugh.

"I could give it to you for safekeeping." Granny patted his arm and he stiffened in surprise.

"Do you mean that, Granny?" he asked.

"Yes. I know it was my own foolishness that made me lose the canvas bag. And truth to tell, it's my fault that the cow got out." Granny thumped her leg. "I wanted to blame you, Wes, but I know I can't do that. It was me."

Wes leaned forward and kissed Granny's cheek. "We're going to find the cow and bring her back. You just rest here and don't worry." He walked toward the door. "Who's going with me?"

The girls looked at each other, then all joined Wes.

"Check near the pines," said Granny. "I saw her heading that way."

"Why didn't you say so before?"

Granny pursed her lips and looked guilty. "I didn't like to admit it was my fault she got loose."

"Aw, Granny!"

"The last time she got out I found her near the pines." She held out her hands. "Don't look at me like that, Wes. I'm just an old, cranky lady who gets mad at people."

Wes walked out with the girls close behind him. He ordered the dogs to stay down, then he faced the girls. "You don't have to help, you know. We can saddle your horses and you can be on your way."

Pam thought about riding the pony and she shivered.

"Just how far away are the pines?" asked Terryl.

"Not too far, but there is a swamp close to them. The swamp monster hangs out there." Wes smiled in a teasing way. "Do you know how many times I heard about the swamp monster from Granny? And I believed her until just a few months ago."

"It sure wasn't very nice of you to scare us with the story," said Terryl.

"Yeah, I know." Wes grinned and the girls laughed. "Come on. Let's go if you really want to," he said.

"We want to," Pam answered before anyone else could say anything.

Together they ran around the barn and crawled through the fence. Dust puffed up onto Terryl's boots as she ran across the pen with the others. She didn't like the idea of going back into the woods, but at least with Wes along they wouldn't get lost.

Just then a movement to her left caught her attention. She squinted against the bright rays of sun to see what it was. "Look over there!" She pointed and the others stopped and looked.

"It's the cow!" Wes shook his head. "I can't believe it. I wonder if she was there all the time."

"There's a calf with her," said Dani.

"No kidding!" Wes looked ready to burst with excitement. "I knew she was going to have a calf soon. I bet she wanted to get off alone to have it. Wait'll Granny sees this!" He ran toward the fence with the girls after him.

Pam caught Terryl's arm and stopped her. "Terryl!" Pam's eyes sparkled and she could barely stand still.

"What?" Terryl wanted to run with the others, but Pam kept her there.

"Terryl, I prayed that we'd find the cow right away for Wes. I prayed! Mom said God answers prayers and he really does!"

Terryl felt funny inside. "It was only a coincidence, Pam."

"Oh, no, I know better, Terryl! I know God answered my prayer." Pam blinked back tears of thanksgiving. She was a new Christian and it was wonderful to see God answer her prayer so quickly and perfectly.

Terryl hid a pleased smile. She was glad that God had answered Pam's prayer. She decided that when they got home she'd ask Mom to tell her more about the Lord. "Let's go help get the cow in, Pam."

They ran to the others and crawled through the fence. Wes showed all of them where to walk so that they could direct the cow and the calf through the gate and inside the pen.

"Don't run or she might spook and get away from us," he said. "Walk slow and easy, and don't shout."

Pam liked watching the black-and-white cow with her small black-and-white calf. The calf was still a little unsteady on its feet, but it followed the cow into the pen. Wes ran to feed and water them while the girls stood at the fence watching.

Several minutes later the girls walked slowly to the barn for their ponies.

"I'll help saddle them and then I'll get Granny," said Wes. He ran to the shed for the saddles. Pam followed to help him. For some reason she liked Wes and liked to be with him. When he smiled at her, she felt good all over.

"Are you sure there isn't a swamp monster, Wes?" Pam lifted a bridle to her shoulder.

"I'm sure," he said confidently.

"We heard a terrible noise in the woods." Pam shivered as she remembered.

Wes grinned sheepishly. "That was me. I was trying to scare you away. I was mad because Dani said I was trespassing."

"You *were* trespassing."

"I know, but I was looking for our cow."

Pam walked across the yard beside Wes. "You should've told us."

"I know. I'm sorry." He stopped and looked down at her. "And I'm sorry for the way Granny treated you."

Pam shrugged. "I wish we would've found the bag." Suddenly an idea popped into her head. "Wes, do you believe that God answers prayer?"

"I guess so."

She told him how she had prayed that they'd find the cow, and he grinned happily. She smiled back and continued, "So, we'll pray that we can find the bag of money for your granny."

"You pray. I don't know how."

"I'm only learning. Mom says praying is talking to God." Pam lifted her eyes heavenward, and spoke quietly. "Thank you, heavenly Father, for helping us find the cow. Now, please help us find the gray canvas bag of money. In Jesus' name. Amen."

Wes grinned. "Thanks."

Pam nodded, then walked with him to the barn feeling taller than the tallest tree in the woods.

TWELVE
Granny Remembers

Suddenly the back door of the house burst opened and Granny stormed out shouting. "Never mind going after the cow. I want every last one of you in the house right this instant! Get them, Wes. Get them in here now!"

"She sounds mad," whispered Pam, shivering.

"She is." Wes groaned. "I guess we'd better get the others and go inside. Maybe when she finds out we already have the cow she won't be so mad."

"I hope you're right." Pam followed Wes inside the barn and dropped the bridle over the saddle that he laid on a bale of hay.

"Girls, Granny wants us inside the house," said Wes in a low, tense voice.

"How come?" asked Sarah, pressing against a stall door, her face ashen. "I'm not going back in that house with your crazy granny!"

"Maybe she wants to thank us," said Pam. Somehow she doubted it, though, judging by the tone of Granny's voice.

"I'm not going!" Sarah folded her arms and shook her head stubbornly.

"I'll stay here with Sarah," said Terryl.

Sarah shook her head harder and frowned. "Don't bother, twin! I can take care of myself!"

Wes walked out of the barn. "Girls, let me talk to Granny alone."

"I don't think she'll make any more trouble," said Pam. "Maybe she found the bag and wants to let us know."

"Let's get it over with," said Terryl. As she ran across the yard she heard the dogs barking inside the house. She swallowed hard and slowed to a walk. It would be very crowded inside the small house with five big dogs and five people. She waited for Wes to walk in first, and followed with Pam and Dani right behind her.

"We found the cow!" cried Wes. "She has a calf."

Granny stood in the middle of the kitchen with the dogs surrounding her. "I don't want to hear about no cow right now! I want to talk about the gray canvas bag! I want to talk about it right now!" Angry fire flew from her eyes. "Start talking, girls, right now!"

Wes moved from one foot to the other. "What's wrong now, Granny? I thought this was settled. I thought we were going to look for the bag by ourselves like we've been doing. You said that. You said you'd buy a safe to put the money in."

"Is that what I said? Did I say all that?" Her face darkened and she stepped one step closer to the girls and Wes. They drew back, suddenly frightened. "Did I say the bag was missing? Did I say that, girls?"

"Granny, what's wrong?" Wes swallowed hard.

"You're acting so funny. What's wrong?"

"Ask them girls, why don't you?" She shook a bony finger at them. "Just ask them girls!"

Pam and Dani stood close together, shivering, but Terryl knotted her fists and jutted out her chin.

"We don't know what you're talking about!" Terryl's voice was loud, even over the panting sounds of the dogs.

"The gray canvas bag!" shouted Grany in a crackly voice. "You know the one I mean! You girls found it and you kept it. That's why it's gone!"

"Granny!" Wes stepped forward and faced Granny squarely. "Don't talk like that! You know what happened. You hid the bag, but you can't remember where. Don't start putting the blame on the girls the way you did on me!"

"You hush, boy! You step back and keep out of this. You can see by those little guilty faces that they took my bag of money."

"No!" cried Pam and Dani.

"How could we?" asked Terryl. She couldn't believe her ears. Just when everything seemed to be going great and Granny was acting rational, this happened!

Granny flung her arms wide. "Didn't you come in my house and pretend to clean it? Didn't you find the money and say, 'Money! Lots of it! We can divide it up and all have some!' Isn't that just what happened in here a while ago?"

One of the dogs lifted his nose and howled. The girls jumped nervously. Terryl wanted to turn and run from the house. "How can you say that about us?" she cried. "Why should we take your money?

We don't want your money! We don't even want to be here!"

Pam plucked at the back of Terryl's shirt to get her attention and make her stop screeching at Granny. Things were bad enough already without Terryl making them worse.

Suddenly Wes stepped between Terryl and Granny. "Hey! Hey, listen to me!" he shouted. His voice cracked as he tried to get their attention. "Granny! Terryl!"

Granny looped a hand around her suspender and glared at Wes, but she kept quiet.

Terryl swallowed hard and rammed her hands deep into her pockets, waiting for Wes to continue.

He took a deep breath, and his face was almost as red as his jacket. "Granny, what are you trying to say? Make sense, will you?"

She nodded, her lips pressed tightly together. She pointed, jabbing her finger toward the living room door. "We'll go in there and then we'll get to the bottom of this!" She strode to the small living room, stepping over the dogs who padded along with her.

Wes hesitated, then motioned for the girls to follow Granny.

Terryl led the way, her boots clomping across the floor. Dani and Pam followed, with Wes just behind them. Pam's stomach fluttered nervously as she stopped near the end table.

Granny pointed to the sofa. "See this?"

Terryl rolled her eyes and shook her head, suddenly impatient to hear Granny's story.

"What about it, Granny?" asked Wes gruffly.

"I lay down on this sofa while you all went to

hunt for the cow." Granny suddenly cocked a brow. "So you found her, did you? And she has a calf?" Before anyone could answer she continued. "So, I lay down on this sofa and then it hit me! I remembered stuffing the gray canvas bag up underneath it in a spot where the lining is torn loose. I cried I was so happy to remember. But when I checked the spot, the bag wasn't there." She narrowed her eyes, looking at the girls. "The bag wasn't there because you girls took it from me. You stole it from an old lady who don't have two beans to rub together!"

"We did not!" cried Dani indignantly. Her cheeks burned and her eyes flashed. "We don't steal!"

"Granny, maybe you were wrong about putting it there," said Wes. "It might have been your last hiding place, before the one where the bag is now."

Granny shook her head. "No. No, no, no, no! I put it there all right. I know that I did as sure as I'm standing here."

The dogs thudded their tails on the floor until Granny snapped her fingers at them, and then they sat like statues.

Terryl and Pam looked at each other. They were thinking the same thing and they knew it. Sarah had cleaned the room. Sarah had thought she'd seen something under the sofa. Terryl had even helped her move the sofa. Sarah could've taken the bag.

Granny hit her fist into her palm with a loud *smack*. The girls jumped. "Now, girls, I want the truth and I want it now!" Granny's eyes widened. "Wait a minute! Wait just one miserable little minute! Where is that other girl? The chubby girl with the black hair cut like boy's hair?"

Terryl spoke up quickly before Pam or Dani could. "She stayed in the barn with the ponies. I'll go get her." Terryl would "get" her all right . . . she couldn't wait to get her. Dani was too nice to do it and Pam too softhearted. "I'll go get her right now," she repeated.

"You do that, twin girl. And you get right back in here with her or my dogs will use you for a play toy!"

Terryl ran from the living room, through the kitchen, and out the screen door. A warm wind blew against her as she ran to the barn, hoping she would find Sarah inside, that she hadn't run off alone to find her way home.

She stepped inside the dark barn, and couldn't see after the bright sunlight outside. The pungent stable odors stung her nose. A cat meowed and a pony nickered a greeting. "Sarah?" she called. "Where are you?"

The calf in the stall bawled and bumped against the door, but Sarah didn't answer, nor come forward.

Anger rushed through Terryl and she stamped her foot. "Sarah, come here right now! I know you can hear me." But could she? Or was she halfway home right now with Granny's bag of money? Terryl stamped her other foot and dust rose up and she sneezed.

She looked around and for the first time noticed that all the tack had been carried into the barn.

Sarah must have done that. Terryl strode to the stall where the ponies were and peered inside. They pressed against the door to greet her, and she touched their noses while she looked in the stall for Sarah. She wasn't hiding there.

Slowly Terryl walked to the piles of baled hay. "Sarah, you come here right now or we'll leave you here alone with all those dogs!"

Sarah popped up from behind a couple of bales of hay. "Scared you, didn't I? You thought I went home, didn't you?" She shot a look around. "Did you bring the dogs with you?"

Terryl shook her head as she studied Sarah thoughtfully.

"Why're you looking at me like that, whichever twin you are?" Sarah backed away until she bumped into a pile of hay.

Terryl reached for Sarah's arm. "I'm Terryl and you're coming with me, Sarah James. You're coming with me right now."

THIRTEEN
A Fight in the Barn

Terryl tugged at Sarah's arm. "We're going to the house to talk to Mrs. Bremer about the bag of money!"

"Oh, no, I'm not! You go by yourself!" Sarah dug in her heels and strained away from Terryl. She was taller and heavier than Terryl. "Let me go right now!"

Perspiration popped out on Terryl's face. "You took that gray canvas bag, didn't you?"

"So? What if I did?" Sarah pried Terryl's fingers off her arm and pushed her away.

Terryl landed with a plop in the middle of the aisle near the ponies' stall. She looked up at Sarah as if she'd never seen her before. Down in her heart she had hoped Sarah was innocent, but now she knew she was guilty. "You *did* take it!"

"So?" Sarah stood with her feet apart and her arms crossed.

"But why?"

"To get even with that crazy old lady! She made me work! She was mean to me and she didn't care if I got in trouble with my dad!"

Terryl scrambled to her feet. "But you knew we

could go home once she had her bag. You knew that! So, why didn't you hand it over to me or to her?"

Sarah swallowed hard. "I looked inside the bag and saw all that money and I wanted to keep it for myself."

"You what?" Terryl's voice rose to a shriek.

"Don't get so upset! She doesn't deserve that money; she lost it. If she'd never found it, it would have just rotted away. So I just fixed it so it wouldn't be wasted." Sarah grinned smugly. "That's all I did."

"Oh, Sarah!" Terryl jabbed her fingers through her tangled hair and pressed her palms to her head. "I can't believe even you could do this! Granny remembered she hid the bag in the sofa! Now she thinks we took it and she's not going to let us go until we hand it over!"

Sarah shook her head stubbornly. "Tell her you don't have it. Let Pam or Dani tell her; they're so innocent that she'll have to believe them."

A spider swung on a web and barely missed Terryl's nose. She brushed it away and asked, "Where is the bag now, Sarah?"

Sarah patted her stomach. "Right here inside my jeans where nobody can get it."

"You know you can't keep it," Terryl said, inching forward.

"I had a hard time zipping my jeans back up. You almost caught me when you came in to help me move the sofa." Sarah tipped back her head and laughed. "All that time we were stacking wood I had the money bag right here."

At that, Terryl flung herself on Sarah and they

both tumbled to the dirt floor, Terryl on top. "Give me that bag! Give it to me right now!"

"No!" Sarah pushed Terryl off and stumbled to her feet, puffing and panting.

Terryl leaped up, her eyes blazing, and rushed at Sarah angrily. Sarah dodged, spun around, and pushed Terryl between the shoulder blades, sending her crashing into a heavy wooden support post. Her head struck the post forcefully, and Terryl slid to the dirt in a crumpled heap.

Inside the house Pam's heart thudded painfully against her rib cage.

"Terryl," she whispered. She was sitting on the floor beside Dani, with her back pressed against the wall. Granny had made them sit down where she could watch them until Terryl and Sarah came back.

"What's wrong, Pam?" whispered Dani, looking worried.

"Terryl needs me! She's hurt!" Pam leaped up, but Dani caught her arm and held her. Pam shook free.

"Sit back down, girlie!" cried Granny from where she sat on the sofa with Wes beside her.

"No!" Pam shook her head and her hair bounced around her face and shoulders. "Terryl is hurt and she needs me!"

Granny frowned. "What kind of story is that? Pure poppycock!" She jumped up and blocked Pam's way. "Get back over there and sit down."

"I can't! Don't you understand?" Color washed over Pam's face, then slipped away, leaving her as white as a ghost. She locked her icy hands together in front of her and trembled so much she almost fell. "Please, let me go to my sister! Please. Oh, please." The last word came out in a sob.

Granny looked helplessly at Wes and at Dani. "What's going on here?"

Wes shrugged and Dani said, "Because the girls are identical twins, they can tell when something's wrong with each other. Pam doesn't make things up; if she says Terryl needs her, then Terryl needs her."

Granny tapped her toe and narrowed her eyes, then finally shrugged. "Then we all go. I don't want no one hurt on my place, that's for sure." She motioned to the dogs and immediately they padded over to her, watching for further orders.

Pam pushed past them and ran for the door, every nerve alive with fear. Sweat trickled down her face and body. Behind her the dogs barked, filling the air with their noise. Pam ignored them, and she ignored Granny's shouts and Dani's anxious questions. All of her attention was focused on getting to Terryl.

She dashed into the barn, hating it that she couldn't see in the semi-darkness. Finally her eyes adjusted and she saw Terryl's crumpled form. With an anguished cry she ran to her twin and dropped to her knees beside her. "Terryl! Oh, Terryl!" Tears filled Pam's eyes and slipped down her ashen cheeks.

The others crowded around them, and the dogs sniffed at the twins.

Terryl slowly opened her eyes. "Pam?" She sat up, moaned, and clutched her head. She could feel a bump the size of a golf ball on her forehead. "Where's Sarah?" she asked weakly.

"Are you all right, Terryl?" Pam touched Terryl's

face and her arm and reached to feel the knot on her forehead. "Oh, Terryl!"

"Where *is* Sarah?" asked Dani, looking around. "Did you find her, Terryl?"

"She was here all right." Terryl stood up with Pam's help.

"What happened in here?" asked Granny, standing with her fists on her thin waist.

Wes walked up and down the aisle of the barn, looking in each stall. His bright red jacket was a distinct contrast to the grayness of the barn.

Terryl leaned on Pam and sighed. "Find Sarah and you'll find your bag of money."

Pam gasped.

"How could she do that?" cried Dani.

Granny slapped her leg. "I knew it! I knew it was you girls that done it!"

"No!" Terryl shook her head, then moaned and held it. "No, it wasn't us. It was only Sarah."

"How can I believe that?" asked Granny, wagging her finger under Terryl's nose.

Pam stepped between Terryl and Granny. Sparks flew from Pam's dark eyes. "Don't you dare talk to my sister like that! She has a bump on her head and she's hurt! None of this would've happened if you hadn't taken our ponies in the first place."

"What?" shrieked Granny.

Wes stepped forward with a red face. "Granny didn't take the ponies; I did. She just took advantage of them being here."

Terryl nudged Pam aside so she could face Granny squarely. "Sarah took the money to get even with you, Mrs. Bremer. So don't blame the rest of us. Now we'd better find Sarah and get your bag back." Terryl raised her voice. "Send the dogs after her to drag her back by the foot!" She waited, listening for Sarah. "The dogs will find her right away, don't you worry!"

Suddenly they heard Sarah scream and looked up to see her peeking down from the haymow. "Don't send the dogs after me. I'll give back the bag!" She held it out and dropped it, and Wes ran to catch it before it hit the floor. He carried it to Granny and held it out to her with a relieved look on his face.

She grabbed it and held it to her heart, then opened it and looked inside. "How do I know if it's all here?"

"Count it," said Wes.

"Right! I'll count it." She glared up at Sarah. "And if one dollar is missing, you'll be very sorry!"

Pam held up her hand. "Wait!" All eyes turned on her and she flushed. "I think we should end our battles right here. Mrs. Bremer, I know Sarah is sorry for taking the bag, but she doesn't know how to say it. And I know you are sorry for keeping us here against our will, but you don't want to say it. I think we should just forget everything that has happened here today so that there won't be any more trouble between us."

Sarah spoke up from above. "I think so too."

"Granny?" Wes nudged her.

She wrinkled her face into a frown, then shrugged. "OK by me. But I still plan on counting this money."

"It's all there," said Sarah. "I didn't take any. Send your dogs outdoors so I can come down."

Granny hesitated, then waved her hand toward the door. At that, the dogs walked outdoors and sank to the ground, their tongues lolling.

Slowly, hesitantly, Sarah crept down the ladder and stood on the dirt floor. She couldn't look at Terryl and Terryl wouldn't look at her.

The ponies moved restlessly as Granny counted out the bills stuffed in the bag.

"It's all here," she said at long last.

"Hooray!" shouted Wes.

"Now we can go home," said Dani, heading for the tack.

Pam's heart froze. It was time to go home—time for her to mount her pony and ride again.

fOURTEEN
Going Home

Pam stood near the fence with Sarah as Dani, Terryl, and Wes led the saddled ponies from the barn into the sunlight. The tightness in her throat made it impossible for her to talk. Just the sight of the ponies made her tremble with fear.

Granny picked up a stick and began to draw on the ground near Dani's feet. "I told you about the wagon track going toward your place. I'll draw a map so you know the way. Can't have you getting lost."

The girls thought about their time in the woods and trembled. They didn't want to get lost ever again.

"You keep right on this dirt road that goes by my place, but don't go as far as the highway—that's too far. Backtrack to here." She pointed with her stick at the map in the dirt. "Two giant white pines stand on either side of the track. The trail goes between them.

"It's a dim trail, but if you know it's there, you'll be able to spot it." She drew the pine trees and a line away from them. "There are trees on all sides, so keep a close look. And don't worry none about

100

the swamp monster." She chuckled and bobbed her head. "But don't you tell my secret, neither. I don't want folks walking around where they don't belong. That swamp monster story works fine to keep 'em away." She went back to her drawing. "Keep following this wagon track until you reach a fence. That fence borders the back pasture of the Big Key. Follow it until you come to your riding trail, then follow that right on home."

"How do you know it goes to the riding trail?" asked Dani.

Granny smiled secretively. "That's for me to know and you to find out."

"Granny," said Wes in a warning voice, then explained, "Granny and I have gone on walks along there with the dogs."

"Dad must've seen your dogs and thought they were wild ones," Dani said. She looked at the dogs lying in the shade of the barn. "I guess he was wrong about them being wild."

"They're my boys," said Granny. She ruffled Wes's hair. "But he's my best boy. Needs a haircut, I see."

Wes ducked away with a laugh. "I told you I did, but you were mad at me and wouldn't listen."

"Being mad was dumb of me, Wes. Real dumb." Wes knew that was as close as Granny would come to apologizing to him, but he accepted it and seemed pleased by it.

He looped the reins over one of the pony's heads, and held a hand out to Pam. "Mount up, Pam." He said, smiling at her, but she was too frightened to respond. She shook her head and pushed Sarah forward.

"Sarah will ride my pony. I'll walk."

"No!" Terryl's voice rang out and Pam turned to her twin in surprise. "Pam, you're riding. Sarah doesn't deserve to. She can walk." Under her breath she added, "Maybe she'll get lost and the swamp monster will get her."

Granny laid a wrinkled, work-worn hand on Terryl's thin shoulder. "Take it from me, girl. Don't hold a grudge. It does more harm than good." Terryl looked at her in surprise, then listened thoughtfully as Granny shared times when she'd hurt others by not forgiving them. While Granny and Terryl talked, Wes pulled Pam aside away from the others.

"Why don't you want to ride, Pam?" he asked, concerned.

She looked into his kind face, her eyes full of fear. "I'm too embarrassed to tell you, Wes."

"Don't be, Pam. I like you, and I think you like me. I mean, we're friends, right?"

She nodded.

"Then tell me."

She peeked at Dani and Sarah who were standing with the ponies near the fence, then she looked down at her boots, and finally up into Wes's face. "I'm scared. I'm not a very good rider." She went on to tell him what had happened earlier in the day. "I might get bucked off or I might fall off again. I don't want to get hurt again!"

Wes studied her thoughtfully. "I guess this is where you find out if God really does answer your prayers."

"What do you mean?" she asked.

"You prayed that we'd find the cow, and we did.
You prayed that we'd find the money bag, and we
did. Now, pray for courage to ride your pony home.
You can do that, can't you, Pam?"

Pam thought about that a long time and finally
nodded. It hadn't occurred to her to pray for
courage, but it made sense. God cared about her
and about every part of her life. He didn't want her
to be afraid of riding a pony. Silently she prayed,
then she smiled at Wes and said, "Fear can't stay in
me now. God is giving me courage to ride again."

"Great! I'll help you mount."

She hesitated, then strode to her pony and
stepped into the stirrup with the aid of Wes's strong
hand. She sat in the saddle and looked around. She
was actually doing it! Once again God had answered
prayer. Under her breath she thanked him for caring
for her.

At long last Terryl turned away from Granny with
a final good-bye. When she saw Pam in the saddle,
her eyes widened in surprise. "You're riding, Pam!
That's great!"

Pam smiled in agreement. Later she'd tell Terryl
how God had helped her.

Terryl swung up into her saddle and looked down
at Sarah. "Ride with me if you want, Sarah."
Granny's talk had convinced Terryl not to hold a
grudge.

Sarah shook her head. "Oh, no! You might pinch
me and push me off or something. I'll ride with
Dani. She's too nice to do anything mean, even if
she is mad at me."

Dani shook her head. "I'm not mad at you, Sarah. Jesus wants me to forgive you, so I have." She held the reins. "You ride in the saddle and I'll ride behind it."

Sarah's round face reddened and a tear squeezed out. "I'm so bad! I know I am. You should feed me to the swamp monster."

"Nonsense," said Granny. "We all do bad things from time to time. But Dani has the right idea. I remember her great-grandma Danielle saying that very same thing, but I guess I forget at times. You've helped me remember, young Dani. Thank you." Granny wiped a tear off her wrinkled cheek with her thumb.

"I'm glad," said Dani, smiling. She waited until Sarah awkwardly climbed into the saddle, then she swung up easily behind her and held the reins. "Maybe we can come see you again sometime, Mrs. Bremer," she said, smiling.

"I'd like that."

"So would I," said Wes, looking at Pam with a wink.

Pam ducked her head and hid a smile.

"'Bye, dogs," called Terryl, lifting her hand to wave. She nudged her pony and followed Dani to the lane that led to the dirt road. Pam rode beside her, smiling a secret little smile.

Suddenly a loud cry rent the air. The girls reined in and turned to stare back to where the cry had come from. Wes laughed and waved his hand.

"That was from the swamp monster," he shouted.

The girls relaxed, turned the ponies, and rode away laughing.

"That was some adventure," said Terryl.

"I don't think I want another one right away," said Pam.

Terryl lifted her head high and flung an arm wide. "I do! I want all the adventures possible! I live for excitement and danger and intrigue! I could face ten swamp monsters! I could tussle with wild dogs and win! Adventure is my game!"

Pam rolled her eyes and laughed. "Oh, Terryl. You are so dramatic, I can't believe you sometimes."

"Me? Dramatic? Never!" Terryl winked at the other girls and they laughed happily as they rode side by side toward the Big Key.